Goosebumps

CREATURE TEACHER:
THE FINAL EXAM

R.L. STINE

SCHOLASTIC

Scholastic Children's Books
An imprint of Scholastic Ltd
Euston House, 24 Eversholt Street, London, NW1 1DB, UK
Registered office: Westfield Road, Southam, Warwickshire, CV47 0RA
SCHOLASTIC, GOOSEBUMPS, GOOSEBUMPS HORRORLAND
and associated logos are trademarks and/or registered trademarks of Scholastic
Inc.

First Published in the US by Scholastic Inc, 2013
First published in the UK by Scholastic Ltd, 2018

ISBN 978 1407 18659 7

Goosebumps books created by Parachute Press, Inc.

A CIP catalogue record for this book
is available from the British Library.

Printed by CPI Group (UK) Ltd, Croydon, CR0 4YY
Papers used by Scholastic Children's Books are made
from wood grown in sustainable forests.

1 3 5 7 9 10 8 6 4 2

www.scholastic.co.uk

WELCOME. YOU ARE MOST WANTED.

Come in. I'm R.L. Stine. Welcome to the Goosebumps office.

Please excuse the mess. I was pickling some pigs' feet for my dinner. But I had trouble getting them into jars, since the feet were still on the pigs.

I had the same problem last week with lamb chops. I didn't know you had to remove them from the lamb first!

I don't really enjoy cooking. I just like to eat living things. I think it's a lot more fun when your food is still moving — don't you?

You are my second visitor today. This morning, my invisible friend came to visit. What a shame. I had to tell him I was too busy and I couldn't see him.

I see you're admiring the WANTED posters on the wall. Those posters show the creepiest, crawliest, grossest villains of all time. They are the MOST WANTED bad guys from the MOST WANTED Goosebumps books.

That poster you are studying is of Mrs. Maaargh. She's a teacher. And yes, as you can see, she's also a monster. That's why her students call her Creature Teacher — but only behind her back.

A boy named Tommy Farrelly can tell you all about her.

Tommy met her at a very strange summer camp, a camp for winners. The problem is, Tommy may not ever return from this camp — unless he can find a way to pass Creature Teacher's Final Exam.

Go ahead. Read Tommy's story. You'll soon find out why Creature Teacher is MOST WANTED.

My name is Tommy Farrelly. I'm twelve, and I wanted to hang around home with my friends this summer. But that's not happening.

My parents are forcing me to go to Winner Island Camp. What kind of camp is that? Well, let me tell you the camp slogan. It's: *Winners Are Always Winners*.

That's right. It's a camp where they teach you how to be a winner.

Now, I'm a totally normal guy. I'm happy most of the time. I do okay in school, mostly A's and B's. And I've got some good friends. So, I don't mean to brag or anything. But I think I'm *already* a winner.

But that isn't enough for my family. In my family, you have to be a **WINNER**. In my family, you have to be the fastest, or the luckiest, or the smartest, or the funniest, or the *best*, day and night.

My dad is a big, strong dude, about a mile wide. He played middle linebacker on his college football team, and they went to the national championship. Now he's football coach at a junior college. All he cares about is *winning*.

My mom is a vice president at a bank. And she's into long-distance bike racing. Sometimes she gets up at four in the morning and rides for sixty miles before breakfast.

Even Darleen, my six-year-old sister, is a superstar. She was reading huge books when she was four. Last year, she won the National Spelling Bee in Washington, DC, against a bunch of high school kids.

Get the picture? I like to chill with my friends and take it easy. How did I get in this family?

And now, here we were pulling up to the dock. In about an hour, the boat was going to come to take me to Winner Island. I saw a little white restaurant near the end of the dock. Above the door, a wooden sign carved like a fish read: ANDY'S FISH SHACK.

The lake sparkled blue and gold. The water rippled gently under bright sunlight. But my parents never take any time to enjoy a beautiful view.

We piled out of the car, and Dad cried, "Race you to the restaurant."

Mom, Dad, and Darleen took off, running as fast as they could. Their shoes slapped the wooden

2

dock. I took one last look at the shimmery lake. Then I trotted after them.

Darleen reached the restaurant door first. "I call the window!" she shouted. She pulled the door open and disappeared inside.

"First one to the table gets the biggest breakfast," Dad said.

Do you see? Everything is a competition in my family.

Andy's Fish Shack was small, with only a few tables. They had red-and-white checkered tablecloths. It was morning, but the restaurant smelled of chowder and fried fish.

A skinny old guy in a sailor's cap and a long white apron was wiping glasses behind the bar. I guessed he was Andy. "Take any table, folks," he called. The place was empty.

Darleen grabbed a seat by the window. I stopped to gaze at the long silvery swordfish mounted over the bar.

"Last again, Tommy," Mom said, shaking her head.

Darleen giggled. "Tommy is always last."

"That's why we're sending him to Winner Island Camp," Dad said. "When he comes back in two weeks, you'd better watch out, Darleen. He'll beat you to the table every time."

She rolled her blue eyes. "No way." My sister has a round face and crinkly blond hair. My parents say she looks like a little doll.

3

That makes her a winner again, since I'm kind of short and chubby, and I wear glasses.

The waiter took our breakfast order. Dad ordered three eggs and an extra helping of bacon to make sure he got the second-biggest breakfast. Mom competes by eating the *least*. "Could I just have the egg whites, please?" she asked. "And no potatoes."

Wind off the lake rattled the window by our table. Outside, I saw a seagull dive into the water.

I had a heavy feeling in the pit of my stomach. "I don't understand why I have to go to this camp," I said. "I mean, seriously."

"It's only two weeks, dummy," Darleen said.

"Don't call me dummy," I snapped.

Mom and Dad like it when Darleen and I fight. They say it shows we both want to win. It shows good competitive spirit.

My parents are weird — right?

"Your sister is right," Dad said. "The camp is only two weeks, but it's really going to toughen you up. You're going to come back a different kid."

Mom pulled the camp brochure from her bag. "Tommy, look what it says. There is a note from Uncle Felix in here. He's the camp director."

She read from the brochure. "When you arrive, you are a LOSER. But losers NEVER leave Winner Island."

Those words gave me a chill. I mean, what does that *mean* — losers never leave? Where do they go? What happens to them?

Guess what? I soon found out. And it wasn't pretty.

Andy set the breakfast plates on the table. Dad grinned. "I win. I got the biggest breakfast."

"But my eggs are the yellowest," Darleen said. It wasn't funny, but Mom and Dad both laughed.

Dad practically emptied a bottle of hot sauce on his eggs. My family puts hot sauce on everything. Not me. I can't stand the stuff.

"I don't *want* to be a different kid when I come back," I said. "I just want to be me."

Darleen gave me a hard shove. "Who would want to be *you*?" she said. Again, my parents laughed as if that was the funniest joke in the world.

"Hey, I see the boat!" Darleen pointed out the window. "I saw it first! I saw it first!"

I turned and saw a white boat, moving fast toward us, bouncing on the blue-green water.

The heavy feeling in my stomach was now a huge rock. "Dad, this isn't fair," I said. "I'm two days late to this camp. It already started. The other kids will have a total advantage over me."

He swallowed a mouthful of eggs. "That's good for you, Tommy," he said. He waved his fork at me. "You'll just have to be even tougher."

"Hey, I finished first!" Mom cried. She showed off her empty plate.

She usually wins the fast-eater prize.

We ate quickly. Dad dropped some money on the table and we hurried outside.

Seagulls screeched and flapped above the little boat as it bobbed up to us. A young man appeared on the deck and leaned over to tie a thick rope around the post on the dock.

His long brown hair fluttered in the wind beneath a red baseball cap turned backward. He had short brown stubble on his cheeks and wore ragged denim cutoffs and a red-and-blue camp T-shirt with the word *Winner* across the front.

He gave me a salute. "Are you Tommy?"

I nodded.

"Welcome aboard. I'm Jared. Jump on. Let's go to Winner Island."

A sharp wave made the boat bounce and tug at the rope.

My family gathered around me. Mom wiped a smudge of egg off my chin.

"Let's say good-bye to the *old* Tommy," Dad said. "Can't wait to see the *new* Tommy." He

7

patted my shoulder. "Let's see who can hug him the hardest."

"No, please —" I started.

Too late. Darleen grabbed me around the waist. She tightened her arms around me with all her strength.

I heard a *craaaaack*. Pain shot up and down my body.

"My ribs!" I cried. "You *broke my ribs*!"

Groaning in pain, I hobbled onto the boat. Dad handed my duffel bag to Jared. He shoved it inside the cabin.

I gazed around, looking for other passengers. But of course, I was the only passenger. Camp had started two days before. We were late because my parents insisted on competing in a barbecue championship in Santa Fe.

The little boat bobbed from side to side. Jared pointed me to a bench seat at the back. "I know it's a lake, but it gets a little rocky, dude," he said. "Don't throw up on the boat, okay? Only losers throw up on the boat."

"Okay," I said, dropping onto the bench. "No problem."

He disappeared around the cabin to the front. A few seconds later, the motor started up with a roar. The boat bobbed away from the dock.

I waved to my family. They waved back. I knew they were about to have their race to the car.

8

They vanished from view as the boat scooted over the lake. The late morning sun sent gold ripples on the gentle waves. The water sparkled all around me. Above the boat, chattering seagulls followed us for a while. Then they gave up and turned back toward land.

Hypnotized by the shimmering gold in the water, I just sat and stared for a long while. My family seldom takes boats anywhere. Mom and Dad say they are too slow. But I found it relaxing to bob on the gentle waves and smell the fresh air.

I saw a stack of camp brochures beside me. I picked one up. It snapped me out of my relaxed mood. I gazed at a photo of the camp director, Uncle Felix. He was bald and kind of mean-looking, with narrow slits for eyes. He had a red bandanna around his neck.

I read another quote from Uncle Felix:

At my camp, you won't just win, you'll win BIG-TIME. We EAT LOSERS for breakfast at Winner Island.

"Whoa," I muttered. I tossed the brochure to the floor.

"It's just another sports camp trying to sound different," I told myself. "And my parents totally fell for it."

I wondered if they had tennis. Tennis and swimming are my best sports. My parents started giving me tennis lessons when I was about as tall as the racket. I'm not a great player. But my forehand is as good as my backhand.

I pulled out my phone. I tried to text my friend Ramon back home. Then I saw that I had no bars. I remembered what the brochure said — no phone or Internet anywhere near Winner Island.

I guess that's part of being tough. You can't complain to anyone about what a loser camp it is.

I stuffed the phone back in my pocket. I gazed around. Nothing but shimmering water on all sides. Like being on another planet.

I pictured the photos of Earth you always see taken from outer space. Nothing but a big blue ball.

How long was this boat ride? Were we almost there?

I stood up and looked for Jared at the front of the boat. But I couldn't see him.

The boat rocked hard. I fell back onto the bench.

I wonder if I'll make any friends at this camp, I thought.

I knew there would probably be a lot of rah-rah, gung-ho types competing to be the best. But maybe I'd find a few kids who were sent there against their will and who thought the whole thing was kind of crazy. Like me.

"Winner Island on the starboard bow!" Jared's voice rang out from somewhere.

I stood up and turned to the front. There it was. I could see the island coming into view. I saw a sandy beach and a row of low, tangled trees. I saw a small dock poking out from the beach. On one side of the dock stretched a green field filled with kids playing some kind of sport.

The motor hiccupped as Jared brought the boat to the side of the dock. The boat tossed up and down, as if it didn't want to be here.

I had that heavy feeling in my stomach again. *Only two weeks*, I reminded myself. *It's only two weeks.*

Jared appeared. His face was sunburned and sweaty. "We made it," he said. "Nice ride, huh? The lake was smooth as glass."

"Yeah. Nice ride," I said.

I heard shouts from the playing field. Jared gave me a boost onto the dock. Then he hoisted my duffel bag up beside me.

"Hope you have a good time, Tommy," he said. His smile faded. He suddenly had this intense look in his eyes. "And hope I see you on the way back."

What does he mean by that?

11

I ducked as a shadow rolled over me. It took me a few seconds to realize it was the shadow of a bird. I raised my eyes and saw a hawk swooping low over the beach.

Jared waved and disappeared into the cabin of the boat. I glanced around, wondering where I was supposed to go. I was still thinking about what he said: *Hope I see you on the way back.*

That wasn't a warning — was it?

"Hey, dog!"

I spun around as a tall, bearded guy in a denim jumpsuit came trotting toward me. He had short, spiky brown hair and silvery eyes. I saw a gold ring in one ear and a sparkly stud on one side of his nose.

"Welcome to Winner Island," he said. He raised a hand for me to slap him a high five. "Where are you from, dog?"

"Hartford, Connecticut," I said.

He nodded. "Okay. Well . . . welcome. My name is Robb. R-o-b-b." He grabbed my duffel bag. "I'll take this to Cabin Twelve for you."

"Thanks, Robb," I said. "Should I follow you, or —"

I stopped when I heard the shouts. Angry cries from the playing field.

Was it a fight during a game?

I turned and squinted at the field, shielding my eyes from the sun with one hand. I gasped when I saw what was happening.

There were dozens of kids, and they were all battling. Shouting and groaning and grunting. Shoving, wrestling, tossing each other to the ground. A huge, horrible free-for-all.

And I saw two counselors — a guy and a girl in red camp T-shirts — standing there with their arms crossed, watching the battle. Just watching. Not trying to stop it.

"Robb, what's going on?" I cried. "They're *killing* each other. Why aren't the counselors stopping it?"

He narrowed his eyes at me. "Stop it? Why should they, dog? That's our morning warm-ups."

My mouth dropped open. "Morning warm-ups?" I squeaked.

I realized my heart was pounding. I'd never been in a fight in my life. I'd never been in a shoving match. I'd never hit anyone, except maybe my sister. And that doesn't count.

Was I going to have to do morning warm-ups, too?

What would I do? Fold myself into a ball on the grass. Yes. *That will be me. I'll be the kid rolling around in the grass, groaning in pain.*

A loser.

Robb tapped my shoulder. "I'll get this duffel bag to Cabin Twelve. You follow that path to Uncle Felix's office. I'm sure he'll want to say hi to you, dog."

I nodded weakly. I was still thinking about morning warm-ups.

I hopped off the dock as Robb headed away with my stuff. The shouts and cries still rang in my ears as I followed the curving, sandy path away from the beach. The path led through a thick patch of smooth-barked trees. On the other side, I saw a bunch of wooden cabins. They were built in a circle around a large meeting area. I saw a burned-out campfire in the middle of the circle. And a bunch of little birds, black with pointy yellow beaks, poking in the dirt around it.

One cabin was bigger and taller than the others. A sign beside the door read STAFF ONLY. I figured that had to be where I'd find Uncle Felix's office.

I stepped inside. I smelled coffee brewing. I saw three office doors in a row along a narrow hall. The door in the middle had a window. The name *Uncle Felix* was stenciled on the window.

I peeked in and saw a small waiting room with three folding chairs lined up against the wall. No one in there.

I pulled open the door and stepped into the waiting room. There was an office at the front of the room. I heard a cough and rustling sounds from the office.

Uncle Felix must be in there.

The door was closed. A sign read: DO NOT KNOCK.

So I took a seat on one of the folding chairs and waited.

And waited.

I could hear the man muttering to himself and clearing his throat on the other side of the door. So I cleared my throat, too, to let him know I was out here.

I gazed at the DO NOT KNOCK sign and waited. And waited some more.

Nothing to read in the room. Nothing to look at. I took out my phone and played *Angry Birds* for a while.

Finally, the office door opened and a man poked his head out. I recognized his bald head and red bandanna from the brochure. Uncle Felix.

He squinted at me. Then he took a few steps into the waiting room. "You're Tommy Farrelly? Are you waiting for me?" he asked. He had a high whistle of a voice.

"Yes," I said, tucking my phone back into my pocket.

He squinted at me some more. "Why didn't you knock?"

I pointed to the sign. "It says not to knock."

He frowned at me. "Well, you failed the first test. A winner doesn't let a little sign stop him. A winner just steps forward and does what he wants."

"Uh . . . sorry," I muttered. What was I supposed to say?

He took a few more steps toward me. He was very short, maybe only a foot taller than me.

And he was skinny with tiny arms and no muscles, and legs that looked like chicken legs beneath his blue shorts.

I can't believe this little wimpy guy runs this tough camp, I thought.

"I'm Uncle Felix," he said in his shrill voice. "You wanted to see me, right, dog? So, you should have ignored the sign and knocked."

He put a hand on my shoulder and guided me back to his office. One wall was covered with photos of campers playing sports. He had a wide desk with nothing on it except for a phone and a pad of paper.

I took a seat in the folding chair in front of his desk. He stood behind his desk and studied me with his tiny black eyes.

"Have you met The Teacher yet, dog?" he asked.

"The Teacher? No. I just arrived," I said. "I know I'm two days late, but my dad said —"

"The Teacher will show you a few tricks," Felix said. "Yes, I know you're a few days behind, dog. But she will whip you into shape."

Whip me into shape?

I took a deep breath. "Why does everyone keep calling me dog?" I asked.

"Because this is a dog-eat-dog camp," he answered. "You'll soon learn. It's eat or be eaten."

For some reason, that made me laugh. *People don't eat people here — do they?*

Felix talked like a tough guy. But he looked like a strong wind would blow him into the trees.

He adjusted his red bandanna. "Well, good luck to you," he said. "You can report to Cabin J now."

I started to stand up — then stopped. "Cabin J? But Robb said he was taking my duffel bag to Cabin Twelve."

Uncle Felix leaned across his desk. "Who? We don't have a Cabin Twelve. Our cabins are all lettered."

"But — but —" I sputtered. "Robb said that —"

"Robb? Who's Robb?" Felix demanded. "No one named Robb works for me."

He paused for a second. I could see he was thinking hard. "Oh, wait," he said softly. "Wait. I get it. Robb. Yes. This guy was having a little joke. Robb."

"Joke?" I said.

He shook his head. "I'm sorry, Tommy. But you've just been *robbed*. Some stranger took all your belongings."

5

I wandered outside to find my cabin. I thought of the words in the camp brochure: *Everyone arrives at Winner Island a loser. . . .*

Well, that definitely described me.

Robbed? Robbed by a guy who said his name was Robb? All of my belongings taken my first minute on the island. How could that happen to me?

Uncle Felix patted my shoulder as I left the staff cabin. "You've learned your first lesson, Tommy," he said. "Don't trust anyone."

I felt kind of dazed. I had a tight feeling in my stomach. Sunlight danced in my eyes. Everything seemed too bright.

I don't even have a toothbrush.

I pulled my phone from my jeans pocket. I had the crazy idea maybe I could call home. Tell my parents to send me all new supplies.

But, of course, the phone was useless here. No bars. No Wi-Fi. I jammed it back in my pocket.

19

Two big yellow dogs, barking ferociously at each other, raced in front of me. I nearly tripped over them.

It's dog-eat-dog here.

They ran through the ashes and blackened logs of the dead fire, and chased each other into the trees.

I heard shouts from the playing field. Insects buzzed around my head. I brushed them away as I struggled to find the path that led to the boys' cabins.

I couldn't find any signs telling me where to go. Maybe this was another test. Find your cabin without any help.

What am I doing here?

The question kept repeating in my mind. I followed a sandy path into the trees. But it ended without leading anywhere. Birds began to squawk. I could still hear the dogs barking somewhere nearby.

"I'm a total loser," I muttered out loud. "I can't even find my cabin."

I tried another path that curved away from the meeting circle. I found myself climbing a gently sloping hill. I could see small, white cabins at the top.

A girl wearing a red camp T-shirt and blue shorts came walking quickly down the hill. She had dark eyes and short, crinkly brown hair under a red baseball cap. She was swinging her arms as she walked.

She stopped when she saw me. Her dark eyes studied me for a moment. "Are you lost?" she asked.

I nodded. "How did you know?"

She pointed behind her. "These are the girls' cabins."

"I'm definitely lost," I said. "I just got here a few minutes ago."

"Two days late," she said, brushing a fly off her knee. "That's not good."

"Do you like this camp?" I blurted out.

She shrugged. "I thought I wanted to be a winner. But —" She stopped and glanced around. She bit her bottom lip. Like she was suddenly tense. "I'm Sophie, by the way," she said.

"Tommy," I said. "I'm . . . looking for Cabin J."

"Huh?" She blinked. "There *is* no Cabin J. The cabins are all numbered."

I stared at her. Was Uncle Felix giving me another test?

"You're the new guy, right?" Sophie said. "Then you're in Cabin Twelve." She pointed past the staff cabin. "Boys are on the other side. There's a path over there."

"Thanks, Sophie," I said.

Her dark eyes darted all around again. "We're

not supposed to help each other," she said in a low whisper. "We're all competing, see. We have to battle each other."

"But . . . why?" I asked.

"So we won't be eaten," she replied.

I laughed. "Dog-eat-dog?"

"It isn't funny," she snapped. "I'm serious. Have you met The Teacher?"

"No. I —"

"You don't have to believe me now, Tommy. But when you meet The Teacher, you'll know I'm telling the truth."

I shielded my eyes from the bright sunlight. "What's so scary about The Teacher?" I demanded.

"The Teacher is a monster," Sophie said. "Her name is Mrs. Maaargh. And no joke. She's really a monster."

I laughed again. "So we're all starring in a horror movie?"

"I'm serious, Tommy. I —"

"I get it," I said. "Let's play a joke on the new kid."

Sophie scowled at me. Her big dark eyes made

her expression intense, serious. But was I really supposed to start believing in monsters?

"I'm trying to help you," she said, balling her hands into fists at her sides. "This camp isn't what it seems to be. We're here to feed the monster."

She was suddenly breathing hard. "You know in the camp brochure where it says only winners leave Winner Island?"

I nodded. "Yeah. I read that."

"Well, it's true, Tommy. Because Mrs. Maaargh *eats* the losers."

I couldn't help it. Something about Sophie's intense expression made me laugh again.

She stepped past me and started to stride down the hill. "I have to go. They're watching us."

"Seriously?" I said.

She spun around. "They're always watching us. To make sure we don't help each other. It's dog-eat-dog, remember? I know you think it's a big joke. But guess who The Teacher is going to eat?"

"Me?"

"Yes. Probably you. Because you're two days late. And you'll never catch up to the rest of us. And you think it's a big joke."

She sighed. "You'll be the loser, Tommy. And you'll never get off this island."

"Give me a break," I said. "Do you really expect me . . ."

24

But she was running full speed down the hill.

I stood and watched her until she disappeared into the trees. *Does she think I'm dumb enough to believe there is a monster on this island? A monster who eats kids?* I thought. *Do I really look like that big of a sucker?*

The sun was scorching my forehead and cheeks. I turned and started down the hill. I passed the burned-out campfire and the staff cabin.

A group of guys came out of the trees. They were walking silently. I saw that they were sweaty and covered in dirt. They walked past me without saying anything.

I found the other path and followed it up a hill. I could see a cluster of white cabins in a clearing up ahead. It took me a while, but I finally found the cabin with the number 12 over the door.

Success.

I pulled open the door and stepped into darkness. I blinked, waiting for my eyes to adjust to the dim light.

But before I could see clearly, a powerful wave of freezing cold water smashed over me, drenching me. It sent me staggering back to the door, spluttering and choking.

"Ohhhhh." I collapsed to my knees, shivering in shock, struggling to catch my breath.

Shaking off water, I made ugly gasping sounds. A big kid came into view. He was holding a metal bucket.

He set it down and leaned over me. His black hair fell over his face. He brushed it back. And I saw the surprise on his face.

"Oops," he said. "Sorry about that."

Huh? Sorry?

He reached out to help me up. "I'm way sorry," he said, brushing his hair back again. "I thought you were someone else."

"Someone else?" Cold water rolled from my hair, down my forehead. My T-shirt was drenched, stuck to my body.

"A dude from Cabin Ten. I thought you were him. We're having a water war."

"W-war?" I stammered.

"He's going to lose," he said. "And I'm going to win. You've got to win here, you know. You don't want to be a loser." He grinned. "A good surprise splash like that will send me to the top of the chart."

I squeezed water from my T-shirt. "I don't know what you're talking about," I said.

"You'll learn." He reached out and pulled me to a sitting position. "I'm Ricardo, by the way. Are you Tommy?"

I nodded.

"Then you and I are bunkmates here. We have this bunk all to ourselves. Sweet?"

"Sweet," I replied.

I glanced around. I thought maybe my duffel bag had been delivered to Cabin 12 after all. But no. No sign of it. "All my stuff was stolen when I got off the boat," I told Ricardo.

His eyes went wide. "Hey, mine too! A guy named Steele met me at the dock and stole my bags."

"Guess they do it to everyone," I said.

He nodded. "Yeah. You've got to be super-tough at this camp. No one gives you a break." He dropped down on the edge of a cot. "Especially the monster."

Not this joke again, I thought.

"You mean the monster that likes to eat all the losers?" I shook my head. "Every camp has stories like that. You really don't expect me to believe —"

I didn't finish, because Sophie came bursting into our cabin. She was panting and looked like

27

she had been running hard. Her face was red. Her dark hair was damp and matted to her forehead.

"Tommy —" she cried breathlessly. "I . . . I'm so sorry."

"Sorry?"

"I . . . ran into Mrs. Maaargh," she stammered. "She heard about you arriving two days late. She — she says she's not going to wait till the end of camp. She's going to eat you *this afternoon*!"

Ricardo's eyes bulged and his mouth dropped open in shock.

Sophie just stood there panting like a dog.

I rolled my eyes. "Does she use silverware?" I asked. "Or will she cut me into triangles like a pizza?"

"This isn't a joke!" Sophie screamed. "What is your *problem*, Tommy? Can't you see I'm telling the truth?"

"When I first came here, I didn't believe it, either," Ricardo said. "But . . . Mrs. Maaargh is no joke."

Sophie dropped down on the other cot. She wiped both hands back through her short, crinkly hair. "Uncle Felix didn't hire her," she told me. "She just showed up on the island. She's here for a free meal. And he's too wimpy and terrified of her to do anything about it."

I still didn't buy it. "You seriously expect me to believe that this monster eats kids?" I said.

29

They both nodded. "Uncle Felix said she could eat one camper. If she promises to let the others go home."

I gazed at them both. They weren't smiling. Their faces were totally serious. They didn't look like they were playing a joke.

They were good actors. But they weren't fooling me.

"Okay," I said. "I've had enough." I turned and started to the cabin door.

"Where are you going?" they both demanded.

"I'm going to find Mrs. Maaargh," I said. "If she exists. And I'm going to put an end to your joke!"

"No! Don't!" they both screamed.

But I was already on my way.

I clenched my jaw and flexed my muscles as I walked toward the staff cabin. *Campers are all supposed to be tough here. Well, okay. I can be tough, too.*

Uncle Felix said to ignore signs. He said a winner does what he wants.

I was tired of being a loser. I hadn't even been in this camp for a full day, and already I was the camp loser. Ready to be eaten by a monster.

No way, I told myself. *Tommy Farrelly is a winner.*

I planned to put an end to this stupid monster story and show Sophie and Ricardo I wasn't a loser.

I saw a crowd of kids outside the circle of cabins. There were at least a dozen, maybe more. And they were all running full speed. Running around and around the circle of cabins, sweat pouring down their foreheads. Their faces were red and tight with panic.

"Why are you running?" I called.

A girl with braids flying behind her head turned to me. "She lets the wolf out at noon!" she shouted. "Don't just stand there — *run!*"

I shook my head. "Wolf?" I muttered. "You've got to be joking.

"Hey!" I jumped back as a bowling ball came bouncing over the grass.

"Can you toss that back to us?" someone called. I turned to see a boy and girl running toward me. "Can you toss that ball back? We're playing dodge ball."

"With a *bowling ball*?" I cried.

They both shrugged. "Don't blame us. Blame Mrs. Maaargh," the girl said.

"Dodge the Bowling Ball is one of Mrs. Maaargh's favorite games," the boy said. "If we don't play, she'll move us down the chart." He picked up the ball and cradled it against his chest in both hands.

"Is *everyone* in on this dumb monster joke?" I demanded.

The girl studied me. "You're new here?"

I nodded. "Just got here."

"You'll learn," she said.

The boy staggered under the weight of the ball. "Want to play? It doesn't hurt too much. Unless it hits you."

"Uh . . . I gotta be somewhere," I said.

I turned and trotted over to the staff building. A short, skinny boy with curly black hair was just walking out. His camp T-shirt hung on his shoulders, ripped to shreds.

He saw me staring at him. "Mrs. Maaargh is in a bad mood today," he said. He held the door open for me. "Good luck," he muttered, as I stepped past him into the building.

I walked down the narrow hall until I came to an office at the far end with the stenciled words on the door: THE TEACHER.

I took a deep breath and pulled back my shoulders. I flexed my muscles.

I'm going to be aggressive.

I'm going to be a winner.

I knocked on the door. I didn't wait for an answer. I pushed the door open and stepped inside.

Sitting at a desk facing the door was an enormous woman, as wide as a truck. She wore a loose-fitting tent of a red dress. Her dark hair was piled a mile high on her head.

My eyes stopped at her huge hands, as big as baseball gloves. They were crossed in front of her on the desk. Her long fingernails were black and curled like animal claws.

And ... and ... she was wearing one of the ugliest monster masks I'd ever seen. Bulging eyes, big knobby warts on her cheeks, rows of pointed teeth in a long animal snout.

Most Halloween stores wouldn't carry a mask that ugly. I wondered where she bought it. But I didn't wait to ask.

I wanted to impress her with how bold I was. I wanted her first impression of Tommy Farrelly to be — "This dude is a WINNER!"

So I gathered all my courage, stepped up to the desk, and cried out, "That's the worst mask I've ever seen. Do you really think you can fool anyone with that?"

And I shot out both hands, clamped my fingers onto the sides of the mask — and started to tug it off her face.

10

"Oh nooooo."

A moan escaped my throat. My fingers dug into warm skin.

No mask. I couldn't find the sides of the mask — because I was *gripping her face!*

Mrs. Maaargh uttered a shrill cry: "You're *hurting* me!"

With a gasp of horror, I forced my hands to spring open. And I stumbled back until I hit the wall.

My heart pounded so hard I couldn't breathe. I could feel my face grow hot and I knew I was blushing bright red. I could still feel the damp, fleshy folds of her face on my fingers.

"Th-that's your real face." The words spilled from my mouth in a trembling voice I'd never heard before. "I . . . I . . . I . . ."

Her eyes bulged, round as onions. She gnashed her pointed teeth. She jumped to her feet, so heavily the whole room shook.

Under the short sleeves of the massive red dress, her arms were like fat hams. She balled her hands into huge fists.

She let out a long, sour breath. The room suddenly smelled like a garbage truck. Her cheeks fell like flabby cookie dough on both sides of her snarling snout.

She didn't blink as she gazed at me. Her brown eyes were wet like swampy pits. "Are you the new dog? Tommy Farrelly?"

"Y-yes." I choked out a tiny reply. I pressed my back hard against the wall.

"Did someone tell you to do this to me?" she boomed. Her bellowing voice made the office window rattle. "Did someone dare you?"

"N-no," I answered honestly.

"Too bad." She licked her brown liver lips with a wide pink cow tongue. "You've made a *very* bad impression on The Teacher."

I lowered my eyes. "Sorry."

"Winners don't apologize," she said.

"Sorry," I replied again. "I just ... didn't believe them when they said you were a monster."

She let out a roar. "You don't *believe* in monsters?"

Another powerful whiff of garbage breath rolled over me. "Well ... I do now." My answer came out in a shuddery whisper.

36

Mrs. Maaargh scratched the lumpy warts on her cheek with the claws on one hand. She squinted at me. "Didn't anyone tell you I'm a bottom-feeder?"

I swallowed. "I'm sorry," I said. "What does that mean?"

"I eat the dog at the bottom of my chart," she said. She stepped up close to me. Her feet made a wet *plop plop plop* sound as she walked.

I glanced down and saw that she was barefoot. Her feet looked like lumpy pillows. She left wet footprints on the floor behind her.

"You'll see my chart later," she growled. "But, guess what? You're there, Tommy. You're at the bottom." A lopsided smile made her doughy cheeks flap. "You're looking like *lunch* to me."

This can't be happening, I thought.

This is the part of the story where the kid wakes up, and it's all been a terrible nightmare.

But I knew this couldn't be a nightmare. *No way* I could ever dream up a monster this ugly or this frightening. Besides, dreams don't stink to high heaven — *do* they?

I have a good imagination. But *no way* I could ever dream up Mrs. Maaargh.

With my back against the office wall, I slid toward the door. My knees were shaking so hard, I didn't think I could stand up much longer. I just wanted to get out of there.

But she bounced past me and blocked the doorway. "You can't leave, dog," she snarled. "You have to be punished."

"Punished?" I whispered.

She nodded. "For hurting The Teacher's face."

"B-but I said I was sorry. I —"

"Sorry isn't enough, dog." Suddenly, I saw a big silvery serving spoon in her hand. I don't know where it came from. But she waved it in front of me.

"Go ahead. Pick my nose, Tommy."

"Huh?" I stared at the serving spoon. It was big. Bigger than a tablespoon. It was the kind of spoon Mom uses to serve mashed potatoes.

Then I raised my eyes to her huge nostrils. They looked like cave openings in the middle of her face.

Mrs. Maaargh shoved the spoon into my hand. "Take the spoon, dog. Quick. Pick my nose for me."

I felt my stomach lurch. I thought I was going to puke.

"Pick my nose. Hurry."

I squeezed the handle of the spoon and stared into the darkness of her nostrils. My hand trembled. My stomach lurched again.

Can I do it?

11

My breath caught in my throat. My hand began to shake as I raised the spoon to her nose.

"Pick it. Pick it for me!" she bellowed.

I could see green drippings in her nostrils. Deep in her nostrils. I forced the spoon a little higher.

Then I opened my mouth in an angry scream: "Noooooooo!"

I tossed the spoon against the wall. Then I lowered my head, swerved around her, and bolted out the door.

I stumbled into the hallway and kept running. The photos on the walls, the office doors and windows — they were all a blur as I stumbled and staggered to the exit.

I shoved open the door with my shoulder. I darted outside. A counselor carrying a stack of Frisbees uttered a cry and dodged out of my way. Frisbees spilled over the ground.

I felt as if my chest was about to explode. But I ran full speed, ignoring the pain.

I sprinted past the running kids. There were dozens of them now, running in a total panic.

I couldn't get the odor of the monster's breath from my nose. Was it clinging to my clothes? And I couldn't get the sight of that green gunky stuff deep in her nostrils from my mind.

I ran past the sports field, into the woods. I could hear the rush of waves in the lake on the other side of the trees.

Where was I going? I didn't know. Wherever my legs took me. I knew I had to get away from Mrs. Maaargh. Get away from Uncle Felix. Get away from the crazy kids, who only wanted to WIN.

This camp was too insane, too dangerous.

Sure, my parents were eager for me to be a winner. But if they only knew . . . If they only knew the truth about this camp, they'd never want me to stay.

My shoes sank into the sand as I stepped out of the trees. I trotted along the beach. No one here. I still had no idea where I was running.

Clouds had rolled over the sky, turning the lake water green and gray. The low waves washed onto the sand. The small dock came into my view.

And I stopped. Panting hard, I stared. The boat. The little white boat that brought me to

Winner Island was back, bobbing at the end of the dock.

Forcing myself to breathe normally, I made my way closer. Was that guy Jared, the guy who piloted the boat, onboard?

I crept to the side of the dock. The boat bumped the wooden pilings gently. I stood perfectly still and listened.

Silence except for the whisper of the wind and the water and shouts from kids back at the camp.

My eyes alert, darting in every direction, I walked down the dock and lowered myself into the back of the boat. "Anyone here?" I called.

No reply.

I can hide in the cabin down below, I decided. *The boat will take me away, take me somewhere safe.*

Then I can phone my parents and tell them to come get me.

I squeezed into the lower cabin. It was very small, smaller than the linen closet at home. But I didn't care. I could make myself comfortable on the cabin floor. I didn't care how long I'd have to wait — as long as the boat took me away from Winner Island to safety.

I settled myself down, crossed my legs, and pressed my back against the cabin wall. My T-shirt was damp from sweat. My glasses were steamed up. My hair was wet, too, matted against my forehead.

I took a deep breath and held it, trying to calm myself. The boat bobbed gently. Then I heard a rattling sound.

Too soft to be the boat motor. Too loud to be crickets chirping.

I sucked in my breath when I heard it again. A long rattle. Like someone shaking a baby rattle. Very nearby.

My muscles tensed. I glanced around the tiny cabin. My eyes stopped on the hand-lettered sign posted on the wall to my side:

WARNING: THIS BOAT PROTECTED BY A VENOMOUS RATTLESNAKE.

I gasped as the rattle grew louder — and I saw a fast, darting flash of movement in front of my face.

12

I ducked.

The snake snapped its jaws inches above my head.

Its tiny eyes glowed as it pulled back its head. The black forked tongue lashed from side to side.

It rattled again, curling its body as it prepared another attack. The rattle grew to a roar in my head.

I froze, hypnotized by the sound, hypnotized by the shiny black eyes.

Then I rolled on the floor as the narrow head shot forward and the fangs snapped again. *Snaaaap.* The fangs missed my ear.

And then as the snake raised its tail to begin its rattle, I leaped to my feet. Off balance, I stumbled headfirst into the cabin wall. Shaking off the pain, I grabbed the rails with both hands and scrambled up the ladder to the top deck.

The snake didn't give up. It snapped again, a few inches from the back of my right ankle.

I kicked at it. Missed.

I grabbed the rail and hoisted myself onto the dock.

Struggling to catch my breath, I took two steps — and bumped into Uncle Felix.

He was wearing a baggy sweatshirt with the words: *Never Cry Uncle*. And baggy blue shorts that made his legs look like toothpicks. He frowned and shook his head at me.

"I — I —" I stammered. I didn't know what to say. "How did you know —?"

"We have cameras everywhere, dog," he said. He pointed to a tiny camera on top of the dock piling. He crossed his arms in front of him. "Listen to me. A winner never quits — and a winner never tries to escape."

"But I want to go home!" I blurted out.

"You want to go home a winner, dog," he said. "Losers never leave Winner Island."

"You *know* about Mrs. Maaargh?" I cried. "You *know* what she does?"

He nodded slowly. "Yes, of course. It's a real shame she came here," he murmured. "I made her promise she'd only eat one kid. That was the best I could do."

"But . . . how can you let her do that?" I cried. "How can you —"

He raised a hand to silence me.

"She's not a bad teacher," he said. "She just gets hungry."

44

He put a hand on my shoulder and started to guide me back to camp.

I stopped and turned to him. "Wh-what are you going to do to me now?" I asked in a trembling voice.

13

"I'm taking you to The Teacher's daily class," Uncle Felix said. "She already knows you tried to escape. I'm sure that will put you at the bottom of her chart."

"I'm already at the bottom of the chart," I muttered.

"Do you know what I always say?" Uncle Felix asked. "A winner tries hard and a loser hardly tries."

He had a million useless phrases. Did he really believe that garbage?

A hideous monster planned to eat me by next week, and he was telling me I should work hard and be a winner.

Why not just pour on the salt and pepper and serve me up on a platter? Hey, Mrs. Maaargh, would you like fries with Tommy?

"You can be a winner," Uncle Felix said as we made our way off the beach. "But you have to do it on your own, dog. No one will help you. Only losers help others. A winner helps himself to whatever he wants."

"Uh . . . thanks for the advice," I said. I tried not to sound sarcastic.

We stepped into the circle of cabins. I saw kids hurrying to the lodge building next to the staff cabin.

Uncle Felix pointed. "That's where The Teacher holds her classes every day." He gave me a gentle shove forward. "Good luck. Don't be late."

I nodded and started to follow the other kids to the lodge. Some kids were racing, competing to see who could get there first. I saw Ricardo and Sophie running hard, side by side.

Then I turned and saw Uncle Felix walking away. He was heading up the path toward the boys' cabins.

He isn't going to his office, I thought.

Suddenly, I had an idea.

"A winner doesn't give up," I murmured to myself. I still wanted to get off the island and away from the horrible camp. Maybe my idea would work.

I stepped up to the staff cabin. I spun around to make sure no one was watching. Then I crept inside.

Two red-and-blue uniformed counselors stepped into an office near the back. They didn't see me. My heart started to pound as I hurried toward Uncle Felix's office.

47

I peered through the window. No one in there. I knew I had to be quick. No way to know how long Uncle Felix would be away.

And if I got caught again . . .

I didn't want to think about that. I just wanted to carry out my plan as fast as I could.

I slipped into the office and carefully closed the door behind me. I gazed up at the ceiling. I didn't see any cameras.

Then I turned to the desk. *Yes!* I didn't imagine it. Uncle Felix had a dark blue phone sitting on the corner of his desk. It had to be the only phone on the island. I remembered seeing it when I first arrived.

I took a deep breath and made a mad dash over to the desk. I glanced back at the office window. No one in the hall. No one to interrupt me.

Now I could call Mom and Dad and tell them what was going on here. Once I told them, I knew they would come for me tomorrow — if not sooner.

Yesss! Yesss!

I grabbed the phone. Raised the receiver to my ear — and screamed, "NOOOOOOOOO!"

14

The liquid felt warm on the side of my face. It came squirting out of the phone and sprayed my cheek.

I was so shocked, I dropped the receiver onto the desk.

I raised my fingers to my cheek, and they came away purple.

My heart was thumping in my chest. I felt my knees start to crumble. I grabbed the side of the desk to keep myself up.

Uncle Felix had a mirror beside one bookshelf. I stared into it and saw the huge purple stain, still wet, on my skin.

The phone had squirted purple ink as soon as I pressed it to my face.

I spotted a stack of paper towels on a table across the room. I darted over to it and began to frantically wipe at the stain.

The purple wasn't coming off. It must have been permanent ink.

I grabbed another stack of paper towels in my trembling hand and ran out of the office. I found a men's room down the hall.

I burst in. Luckily, no one was in there. I soaked the towels in the sink and began dabbing and wiping at the stain. But no. One side of my face was purple now. And the purple was not coming off.

I really am in trouble, I decided.

Now everyone will know what I tried to do. I am totally doomed.

I had no choice. Every camper was at Mrs. Maaargh's class. I had to go, too. I had to go with my big purple blotch.

I dried off my face and walked out of the staff building. *Maybe this is lucky. Maybe Mrs. Maaargh doesn't like to eat purple food,* I told myself.

Good, Tommy. You can still joke. Even when you're about to become monster meat.

I stepped into the classroom. Mrs. Maaargh was pinning something on the wall and had her back turned. I spotted an empty seat in the last row. I tried to keep the purple side of my face hidden from everyone as I edged my way sideways down the row of chairs.

As I made my way to the back, I saw two other kids — a boy and a girl — with purple stains on their faces. Did that make me feel better? Not much.

50

I dropped into the empty seat and covered my cheeks with my hands. I saw Sophie in the front row. She had turned around and was staring hard at me. I pretended I didn't see her.

Ricardo sat at a desk by the window. He was gazing at a squirrel on the grass. He turned to the front when Mrs. Maaargh cleared her throat. It was a disgusting sound, like someone puking her guts out. But it got everyone's attention.

She picked at one of the knobby warts on her nose. "We have a new dog in class," she told everyone. "Tommy Farrelly. He's the one in the back row trying to hide the fresh purple stain on his face."

A few kids turned to stare at me. But most of them stayed silent and kept their eyes on Mrs. Maaargh.

"For the benefit of the new dog," she continued, "I'm going to go over what we're doing here."

And then she belched really loudly. A long, vibrating burp that sounded like a sewer exploding. The kids in the front row all cringed and ducked as her smelly breath rolled over them.

"That's the last time I eat raccoon for breakfast," she said. She shook her head. "That raccoon was overcooked."

She swallowed loudly. "To begin at the

51

beginning, I am called The Teacher. That's because my job is to teach you what you need to know. And what you need to know is . . . you'd better keep The Teacher happy."

She pointed a fat hand at the sheet she had just hung on the wall. "As most of you already know, this is my Wait Watchers Chart. It means we will all wait and watch to see who I will eat on the last day of camp."

I squinted at the chart. It seemed to have the names of all the campers on it.

"I never send home the biggest loser at the bottom of the chart," she said. "Parents send their kids here to be winners. And it wouldn't be fair to them to send a loser home. So I eat the kid instead."

A few kids shifted uncomfortably in their seats. But no one made a sound. Ricardo had his hands clasped tightly in his lap. He stared hard at the chart.

I saw his name. It was somewhere near the middle. Unless he totally messed up, Ricardo was pretty safe.

Mrs. Maaargh bent down and picked something off the floor. It looked like some kind of fat insect. She popped it into her mouth and chewed it for a while.

Then she pulled the chart off the wall and held it up so everyone could see it.

No big surprise. My name was at the bottom. The super-big loser of the summer.

To my surprise, Sophie's name was next-to-last, right above mine.

I saw the shock on Sophie's face. She went pale. "Mrs. Maaargh?" She raised her hand.

"Mrs. Maaargh?" Sophie called out again. "Why am I down at the bottom?"

"Because you were seen helping Tommy," Mrs. Maaargh answered. "Remember, Sophie — you know what Uncle Felix always says. A winner fights to win. A winner never helps a loser. That's the fastest way to *become* a loser."

Sophie scrunched her face up angrily. I saw her ball her hands into tight fists. But she didn't say another word.

Mrs. Maaargh set down the chart. "We have a lot of time left for camp," she said. "I can't wait to see which one of you will join me for lunch!" She tossed her head back in an ugly laugh, enjoying her own joke.

"I'm going to give you several tests as part of the Final Exam," she said, when she finally stopped laughing. "The tests will let us see who at this camp is tough. Which of you will do *anything* to beat the other campers."

An ugly grin sent the folds of her face shivering. "Today, we will have an Earth Science experiment."

She reached into a desk drawer and pulled out a long, fat purple worm. She dangled the worm high so everyone could see it, and her grin grew even wider.

"Let's see how many of these you can eat."

15

Kids moaned and groaned. I had a sick feeling in the pit of my stomach.

I gazed at the long worm dangling from Mrs. Maaargh's clawed hand. It gleamed wetly under the bright ceiling lights. *It's at least six inches long*, I thought. Did she really want us to eat worms that big?

I knew the answer. So did everyone else in the class. She was a monster. She didn't care if we choked on worm meat or not.

We were there to prove we were winners. I knew the other kids would do *anything* to keep from taking my place at the bottom of her chart.

Down the row of desks, I saw Ricardo raise his hand. "Mrs. Maaargh? Does it matter if we eat the head first or the tail first?"

The thought of gulping down one of those wet purple things made my stomach lurch. I pressed my hand over my mouth to keep my breakfast from spewing.

Mrs. Maaargh pulled a large red bowl from under her desk. I could see worms curling over the top of it. She climbed to her feet and carried the bowl to the front row of kids. Her huge, pillowy bare feet made a squishy, *plop plop plop* sound as she walked.

"Eat them any way you like," she said. "You can put a cherry on yours, if you like. I'm giving each of you a worm. They're nice and cold. I kept them in my fridge."

She handed a worm to the first girl in the row. It slid out of the girl's fingers and dropped onto her desktop.

"You have to squeeze them to hold on to them," Mrs. Maaargh scolded her. "Hold the worm high over your open mouth. When I blow my whistle, let go. Drop them into your mouth and chew them up or swallow them whole."

Kids groaned again. Mrs. Maaargh moved down the row, handing out wriggling worms.

This is totally sick, I thought.

I saw Sophie take her worm. It tried to curl itself around her wrist. She had to pull it off in order to hold it over her mouth.

Sophie stared hard at her worm. Her hand didn't tremble. I could see she was determined to eat the worm. She didn't like being so close to the bottom of the chart.

The boy next to her looked sick. His face

was actually green. But he took the worm from Mrs. Maaargh and gripped it tightly in front of him.

"Some of these worms still have dirt clinging to them," Mrs. Maaargh said. "Sorry I didn't do a better job of cleaning them off."

She handed me a very long one. It had chunks of brown dirt up and down it.

I pinched one end and held it up. The worm twisted and wriggled and tried to get free.

My stomach heave-ho'd again. I was having trouble keeping my breakfast down. Glancing around the room, I saw that other kids had the same expression on their faces.

One girl covered her eyes with one hand while she held the worm in the other. The dude next to me was hyperventilating, panting like a dog. His chest heaved up and down. His hand trembled in the air, making the worm swing from side to side.

Mrs. Maaargh blew the whistle.

A heavy hush fell over the room. The whistle still rang in my ears.

Kids held their worms high. But no one moved to be the first to drop the worm into their mouth.

My chest tightened in panic. My skin suddenly tingled as if an electric charge was shooting through me.

57

I was desperate. Desperate to do something right. I *had* to climb off the bottom rung of the chart. I *had* to be a winner.

I held my breath. I swung the worm over my mouth.

Can I do it? Can I swallow it?

16

Yes.

I opened my fingers and let the worm drop.

I almost missed my mouth. The worm hit my cheek and started to crawl.

I inhaled hard — and sucked the worm inside. It felt cold and wet on my tongue. And I could feel the clumps of dirt on its skin.

Choke it down. Choke it down, Tommy.

I started to gag. I made a loud choking sound. I gagged again.

It wouldn't go down. I couldn't force it down.

Then finally . . . finally . . . the worm scraped the back of my tongue and started to slide.

Ohhhhhh. It tasted sour. So bitter.

I made a gulping motion and it slid the rest of the way. Off the back of my tongue and down my throat.

Oh, wow.

I pressed both hands over my stomach to try to make it stop churning and bubbling.

I did it! Success!

It was the most disgusting thing I'd ever done in my life. But I swallowed the thing. Did that make me a winner?

I gazed around the room. Silence. To my surprise, kids were staring at me.

And then another surprise: They were all still holding on to their worms.

Huh? What's up with that?

Ricardo lowered his eyes and shook his head sadly. Sophie frowned at me.

"You failed, Tommy." Mrs. Maaargh's raspy voice made me jump. The folds of flesh on her cheeks rumbled as she shook her head at me. "I should have known you'd be the one."

Failed?

"I — I — I don't understand," I choked out. I still had the metallic taste of the worm on my tongue. "What do you mean?"

Everyone watched me in silence.

"Tommy, this was a test of courage — remember?" Mrs. Maaargh said. "It was a test to see who in this room had the courage *not* to eat an innocent earthworm. Anyone who would eat an earthworm is a *loser*."

"But — but —" I sputtered.

Everyone else in the class still held on to their worm. Everyone but me.

"Everyone showed courage but you," Mrs. Maaargh growled.

60

"But it took courage to swallow that thing!" I cried. "I nearly choked on it and —"

"Look at your classmates," she said. "Look how much *more* courage they showed by *not* following my instructions."

I realized there was no way I could argue with her. I watched her fiddle with some names on the chart. You-know-who stayed on the bottom. Yours truly, Tommy the Loser.

She held up the big bowl. "Pass your worms to the front. Good job, everyone."

It took a minute or two to collect all the worms. Then she walked over to a table at the side of the room. "That test made me hungry," she said. "My stomach is growling like a hungry grizzly bear."

I saw a glass cage on the table. There were little white creatures with long pink tails crawling around inside it. White rats.

Mrs. Maaargh lifted the cage lid. She reached in and pulled out a white rat by its tail.

It squeaked as she dropped it into her mouth and chewed it up noisily. She chewed for a long while, a big smile on her face. Then she swallowed it with a loud *gulp*.

"I like them plain," she said, wiping her flabby lips with the back of one hand. "I hate spicy food, don't you? It doesn't agree with me at all. I guess I have a sensitive stomach."

A sensitive stomach? She just ate a rat, and she says she has a delicate stomach?!

61

I knew I should shut up, but I couldn't help myself. "Mrs. Maaargh," I said, "you said I shouldn't eat an innocent worm. But you just ate an innocent white rat."

Some kids gasped. I guess they thought it wasn't smart to argue with The Teacher.

"Yes, I know, Tommy," Mrs. Maaargh rasped. "But I have an excuse. I'm a MONSTER."

She tossed back her head and laughed so hard, chunks of the rat came flying out of her mouth.

That evening after supper, Ricardo and I were trying to relax in our cabin. He hunched on one cot, and I sat across from him on the floor, my back against the wall.

Crickets chirped outside the cabin window as the sun lowered itself behind the trees. The air grew cooler. I could hear the beats of someone's music far down the hill.

"Why did your parents send you here?" I asked Ricardo.

He rubbed some mosquito bites on his arm. "It was my dad's idea," he said. "He's a big-deal money guy. He has these fancy offices on Wall Street. I don't really know what he does. But he says he makes a ton of money for people."

I shifted my weight on the floor. "And he sent you here because ...?"

"Because he says you have to be a total winner to make money on Wall Street. He says you have to be able to compete against anybody so you can win win win. So when he saw the ad for this camp, he signed me up that day."

Ricardo sighed. "There's only one problem. . . ." His eyes gazed out the window.

"Which is?" I asked.

"I don't want to be like him. I don't want to be a money guy on Wall Street. I don't want to win win win."

"What do you *want* to do?" I asked.

He shrugged and scratched his bites some more. "I don't know. I'm just a kid, right? How should I know? Do *you* know what you want to do?"

I snickered. "For sure. I have big plans. My plan is to be eaten by a monster at the age of twelve."

His expression turned serious. "Good you can joke about it," he murmured.

"What else can I do?" I said. "Everything I do here is wrong. *No way* I can pull myself up from the bottom of the chart."

"Seriously," Ricardo said. "You got off to such a bad start with Mrs. Maaargh. It's like she already made her mind up."

"Tell me about it," I muttered. "I'm doomed. Totally. There's no way off this island. And no way to call home or get a message out or anything."

"Your face is still purple," Ricardo said. "At least you weren't the first kid to try to phone home."

"Hey, dudes!" Sophie poked her head in the door. She stepped in. She had a red-and-white polka-dot bandanna tied in her hair. She wore a dark sweatshirt pulled down over white tennis shorts. "What's up?"

"Not much," Ricardo muttered.

"We're talking about how much we love this camp," I said.

Sophie dropped beside me on the floor. "Seriously. Let's all sing the camp song together."

I gave her a shove. "Is there really a camp song?"

She straightened her bandanna. "For sure. Don't you know it?" She started to sing: *"Don't come unglued . . . or you'll end up as food. . . ."*

I groaned. I suddenly didn't feel like joking anymore. I swallowed hard. "That ugly monster really is going to eat me next week. And we're sitting here talking like everything is normal."

Sophie grabbed my arm. "That's why I risked coming up here, Tommy. I hope no one saw me. I have an idea for you."

"An idea?"

She nodded. "I have an idea for how you can get on Mrs. Maaargh's good side. You can bring her flowers."

I jumped to my feet. "Are you totally nuts? Do you really think —"

She raised a hand to shut me up. "Just listen to me. Give me a chance. I think this will help you. Really."

I crossed my arms in front of my chest. "Okay. Go ahead. Talk."

"There's a big patch of beautiful wildflowers in the middle of the island," Sophie said. "Go pick some tomorrow morning. Bring Mrs. Maaargh a big bouquet of flowers. And tell her you want to apologize for the bad start you got off to here. She'll be touched. She really will."

"She'll just *eat* the flowers," I said. "She'll eat the flowers as an appetizer before she eats me."

"Hey, dude, it's worth a try," Ricardo said. "What have you got to lose?"

I sighed again. "You're right. What have I got to lose?"

"She can only eat you *once*, right?" Ricardo said.

"Thanks for cheering me up," I said.

"Just don't let anyone know I helped you," Sophie said. She peeked out of the cabin, glanced both ways, then disappeared.

The next morning, I went off in search of wild-flowers. I had a good feeling about this. I thought maybe I could change Mrs. Maaargh's opinion of me.

Guess how it worked out.

18

It was a hot summer morning. The air felt sticky and wet. Waves of buzzing white gnats flew over the camp.

I didn't eat much breakfast. I choked down a dry piece of toast and half a glass of pulpy orange juice. I guess I was too excited about my mission to find Mrs. Maaargh a wildflower bouquet.

The first activity of the morning was Sports Hour. Counselors called the guys to the playing field near the beach. We had a choice of Full Contact Tackle Chess or Dodge the Javelin.

I stayed back by the trees and watched the guys choose up sides. When I was sure no one was watching, I turned and darted into the darkness of the woods.

I moved quickly, listening for someone to shout out, to call me back. But their voices faded behind me as I trotted through the tangled trees. Tree frogs croaked loudly in the limbs above my head. I kept stumbling over fallen branches and upraised roots.

Glancing up, I saw several big blackbirds lined up on a low tree branch. They all had their eyes on me. Their ragged wings were pulled back as if they were planning to swoop to the attack.

I shivered and hunched my shoulders as I ran under the branch.

Something scuttled over my feet. Too big to be a squirrel or rabbit. I squinted down at it, but it vanished into the carpet of brown leaves.

This island is creeping me out.

Another group of large blackbirds began to squawk in a nearby tree. I spun around. The camp was far behind now. I was surrounded by smooth-barked trees and shrubs with vines like tendrils.

I couldn't hear any voices from the camp. The only sounds were the cries of the birds and the crunch of dead leaves under my shoes.

Sophie said there was a clearing with a wide patch of wildflowers in the middle of the island. I wondered how long I had to make my way through these hot, damp woods before I found it.

I was breathing hard, my T-shirt soaked to my back, when the clearing finally came into view. I stopped at the edge of the trees and shielded my eyes with one hand from the sudden splash of bright sunlight.

Sophie hadn't made it up. I stared at a wide circle of flowers so bright the colors vibrated. Blues and purples and yellows, all tumbling over each other. Waving in the hot breeze and shimmering under the cloudless sky.

I took a few steps to the edge of the wildflower patch. As I came closer, I saw bees hovering over the blossoms, and fluttering white butterflies, and even a hummingbird or two.

I'm not a big flower person. My dad competes in a flower show each year. And, of course, he has to grow the biggest, best plants in the show and win all the blue medals. Win win win.

He'd go berserk if he saw these flowers. They were so much more beautiful than his.

I bent down and started to pick some. I decided to gather three or four different colors. Bees buzzed out of my way as I wrapped my fingers around the stems and tugged them up. The ground was soft. They lifted easily.

It didn't take long to have a nice bouquet. They smelled so sweet. I held them in one hand and brushed a bee away with the other. Then I turned and started back to camp.

The woods confused me. For a while, I thought I was lost, making the same circle in the trees. Finally, I remembered to keep the sun behind me. And I found my way easily.

The Tackle Chess match was still going on.

Guys were grunting and groaning over a big chessboard, tackling each other after every move.

I kept to the trees until I came to the circle of cabins. I ducked behind a tall shrub when I saw Uncle Felix. He was carrying a javelin in one hand, swinging it as he walked. The javelin was almost as tall as he was.

I wondered how the Dodge the Javelin competition went. Thinking about it made me shudder. The loser could go home with a big hole in his body.

I waited till Uncle Felix was out of sight. Then I made my way into the staff office building. My hand trembled. I nearly dropped the bouquet.

I was happy to see Mrs. Maaargh in her office. I knocked on the door, then stepped inside.

My heart started to pound. This was my big chance. I didn't want to blow it.

This has to work.

I stepped up to her desk. "I — I thought you might like these," I stammered. And I pushed the big bouquet of wildflowers into her hands.

19

Mrs. Maaargh jumped to her feet. She gazed down at the bouquet in her hands, and her eyes bulged until they were as big as tennis balls.

"*Uurrrrrrk.*" She opened her mouth in an ugly groan. "*Urrrrrrk.*"

Then she tossed back her head and let out an explosion of a sneeze that shook the room. The flowers flew from her hands and scattered over her desk and the floor.

She sneezed again.

"*Uurrrrrrrrrrk!*" Another groan from deep in her throat.

And then a sneeze so powerful I thought her head had exploded.

Enormous gobs of yellow snot splattered the office walls. Another sneeze sent a thick puddle of snot to the ceiling. It stuck for a moment — then dropped onto my head.

"Ohhhh." I slapped at the sticky, yellow goo

71

with both hands. It dripped down my forehead and the back of my head.

I started to shake. One more giant snot blast in my face, and I wouldn't be able to breathe.

Mrs. Maaargh's eyes spewed tears. Her fat face turned purple. She sneezed another splat of yellow snot onto the office door.

Her whole body heaved and shook. Finally, she wrapped her arms tightly around herself, held her breath — and the sneezing attack ended.

I was still trying to wipe the sticky snot from my hair and face. "Let me guess," I said softly. "You're allergic to wildflowers."

Her eyes bulged again. Her face turned an even darker purple. She bared her rows of pointed teeth — and roared.

It was an animal roar. A *monster* roar. She tossed back her head and bellowed in a total rage.

I spun around. My legs were like rubber bands. I couldn't get them to work.

Somehow I staggered to the office door. The doorknob was covered in yellow snot. But I grabbed it, pulled the door open, and lurched into the hall.

I could hear her animal wails of fury all the way down the hall, out the building, and up the path to the boys' cabins. The cries rang through the air like ambulance sirens.

That didn't go well.

I'm in trouble.

I'm . . . doomed.

Gasping for breath, my chest throbbing, I burst into my cabin. I stopped at the door when I saw Ricardo and Sophie inside.

Ricardo was wiping mud off his face with a bath towel. He must have been Mud Boxing, one of the other competitions. When she saw me, Sophie jumped up from the cot she had been sitting on.

"You knew she was allergic. You tricked me. I — I thought you were my friends," I stammered breathlessly.

"We *are* your friends," Sophie said. "We were trying to teach you not to trust anyone."

"Don't you understand?" Ricardo said. "We're your friends. But you can't trust anyone here. *Especially* your friends."

Does that make any sense at all?

I slumped onto my cot. My hair was sticky with yellow snot. My whole body prickled with sweat. My heart was still racing in my chest.

"But . . . what if we all worked together?" I said. "What if we all stood up to Uncle Felix and Mrs. Maaargh and refused to play their game?"

They both stared at me as if I was speaking a foreign language.

"That idea is for losers," Sophie said finally. "We came here to be winners."

"Dog-eat-dog," said Ricardo.

I scowled at them both. "I get it," I muttered. "I can't trust either of you. I can't trust anybody here."

Suddenly, the cabin door slammed open. Startled, I jumped to my feet as two big dudes — counselors in red WINNER T-shirts — burst in. They both had shaved heads, biceps bulging under their T-shirt sleeves, and mean expressions.

Their eyes moved from face to face and stopped on me. They each grabbed one of my arms.

"You're coming with us," one of them growled. They started to drag me to the door.

"Hey — let go!" I cried. "Let go of me! Where are you taking me?"

20

They didn't answer my questions until they'd pulled me down to the mud pit on the beach. It was the size of a small pond, filled with gooey brown mud. When you stepped into it, you sank instantly to your waist.

"Why did you drag me here? What's the big idea?" I cried.

"You missed Sports Hour," one of the beefy, bald counselors said. "So how about a game of mud tag?"

"Huh? Mud tag? No. I —"

"Only losers run away," his buddy said. "It's time for your mud tag game. Go ahead. Try to run. Then we'll tag you."

"No — please," I begged. "Mud makes me break out. Really."

I turned to see Mrs. Maaargh watching from the other side of the mud pit. Her head was still swollen from the wildflowers. She had chunks of yellow snot in her hair.

She was leaning on a javelin and had a big grin on her puffy face. "Let's see how you do in the mud, dog," she said.

"But I don't want —"

"Bert here will give you a good game," she said. She signaled Bert with one paw.

My heart leaped to my mouth. I started to choke. "No. Please —" I begged.

Bert nodded and came after me. His hands were bigger than my head!

I stopped at the edge of the mud pit. The wet mud was actually bubbling.

Bert came staggering after me, hands raised to tag me. "You know how to play tag, don't you, dog?"

I had no choice. I stumbled into the pit — and instantly began to sink. The warm mud seeped over my sneakers and up my legs.

Bert stepped into the mud pit. He had one blue eye and one brown eye. They were both staring at me as if they could see right through me.

It was a very short match.

Before I could move, Bert swung his arm forward and gave me a hard slap in the gut. "Tag — you're it!"

I doubled over. Collapsed face-first into the mud. And just sprawled there, my arms out-stretched on the warm mud, waiting for the pain to stop racing up and down my body.

Game over.

Lying there, facedown in the mud, frozen in pain, I knew what I had to do. I knew the only way I could possibly survive.

21

I took a long shower to wash the mud off. I'm not sure I got it all. My ears were still clogged, and clumps of mud kept dripping from my hair.

I knew my stomach would stop hurting in a week or two. Of course, a little stomach pain wouldn't matter if I was Mrs. Maaargh's lunch.

Eight days. Only eight days to go at Camp Winner.

I left mud stains on the towel as I dried myself off. Then I wrapped the towel around my waist and walked up the hill to my cabin.

Someone had painted three words in red on the side of the cabin: MONSTER MEAT INSIDE.

I didn't care. I had made up my mind. As soon as Bert's "tag" sent me toppling facedown into the mud, I knew what I had to do to survive.

Hide.

Yes, I'd tried it once before. On the boat. The rattlesnake and Uncle Felix's spy cameras made that a major fail.

But I planned to be smarter this time. I planned to find a place where there were no spy cameras. I planned to hide on the other side of the island, past the clearing of wildflowers.

There had to be a cave there. Or maybe an abandoned cabin or cottage. Maybe just a dock I could hide under and wait for the boat to come back and take me off the island.

Maybe I'd find a canoe or even a motorboat. I could take *myself* off the island and get to safety on the other side of the lake.

These brave thoughts made me feel a little better. I pulled on a fresh pair of camp shorts and a T-shirt. I didn't have anything to pack or take with me since all my belongings had been stolen.

I remembered that Ricardo had some candy bars hidden under his bed. I ducked down, pulled a few out, and tucked them in my pockets.

What else would I eat for eight days? I didn't want to think about that now. I just wanted to get out of there.

I started to the door when Ricardo came walking in. "Did you see what someone painted on the cabin?" he asked.

I rolled my eyes. "Yeah. Nice."

He wiped his sweaty face with the front of his T-shirt. "How did you do in mud tag?"

"How do you think?" I said. I didn't want to talk to him. Especially after the mean trick he and Sophie had played on me.

"You make us all look good," he said. He pulled the shirt over his head and tossed it into a corner.

"Thanks a bunch," I said. I moved past him toward the door.

"Where are you going?" he asked, scratching his armpits. "Class starts in a few minutes."

"Nowhere," I said. "I'll be right back." *No way* I would tell him my plan. I knew he wasn't a friend.

He laughed. "You still have some mud behind your ears."

I ignored him and stomped out the door. I was surprised to see that dark clouds had rolled over the island. The air was heavy and moist. It was about to storm.

I didn't hurry. I walked slowly down the hill. I kept my eyes straight ahead and pretended to act normal. You know. Casual. I didn't want anyone to suspect that I was running away.

Most kids were in their cabins, cleaning up from the morning sports activities, getting ready for class. I saw Mrs. Maaargh wobbling to the classroom on her huge, pillowy feet. Her red polka-dot dress ballooned around her in the wind, making her look like a monster-sized ladybug.

Luckily, she didn't see me.

I let out a long sigh as I made it to the woods. I felt a few cold raindrops on my forehead. But I didn't care. I was doing it. I was escaping.

I followed the path that I'd found my last time in the woods. With the storm clouds overhead, the woods were nearly as dark as night. Tall shrubs twisted and bent like living creatures. The trees creaked and groaned, as if trying to tell me to go back.

No way. I knew I had to make this plan work. If it didn't, just put a fork in me and call me cooked.

Thunder rumbled in the distance. Rain pattered the tree leaves like drumbeats.

I squinted through the dim gray light, through the shifting shadows. I needed to find some kind of shelter. A cave, a cabin, a shack, even a hollow tree.

I was getting soaked. The air had turned cold. Wind shook even more rainwater down on me from the high tree branches.

I shivered. I was nearing the end of the path. Nothing but tangles of trees and shrubs up ahead.

I wiped rainwater off my forehead. And cried out as I stumbled over something hard and wide.

I landed on my knees. And stared at the dark object in front of me.

"I don't believe it!" I cried. "What's *this* doing here?"

22

My duffel bag.

I checked the name tag on it just to make sure. Yes. It was mine. That dude Robb just dumped it here in the middle of the woods.

Squatting over it, I pulled it open. My clothes were neatly folded at the top. Robb hadn't stolen anything. He hadn't even opened it. He'd just left it here.

Thunder echoed off the trees. The wind swirled around me.

I decided to go back to the cabin. I was happy to have all my stuff back. I could try to escape again when the weather was better.

I swung the duffel bag over my shoulder and carried it to my cabin. Ricardo looked up from a book he was reading as I walked in.

"Where were you?" he demanded. "You weren't in class. Mrs. Maaargh said she hates it when her food runs away."

"I found my stuff," I said. "Look. Everything

is there. That guy didn't steal a thing. My bag was in the woods."

"You were in the woods?" Ricardo asked. "Why? Were you running away?"

I ignored his questions and started to unpack the bag. I jammed my T-shirts into the one dresser drawer that was mine. And I hung my two pairs of jeans on a hook on the far wall.

Then I pulled something from the bottom. It was wrapped tightly in newspaper. I tore at the tape and pulled the wrapping off. And stared at the slender bottle in my hand.

"I don't believe my parents packed this!" I said.

Ricardo set his book on the floor and walked over. "What is it?"

I held the bottle up to him with my hand wrapped around the label. "It's my favorite chocolate sauce," I said. "It's awesome."

He eyed the bottle. "Chocolate sauce?"

"It's sort of cherry-chocolate," I said. "You won't believe it. Here. Try a taste."

I twisted open the lid. I held it over his mouth. And I poured a little onto his tongue.

It took him a few seconds to react. Then his eyes went wide and he let out a shrill scream.

"It's *burning* me! Noooo. It BURNS! It BURNS! I — I can't breathe! Help me! Can't BREATHE!"

23

Screaming and choking, Ricardo dove for a water bottle beside his cot. He tore it open and glugged down the whole bottle.

I laughed, enjoying my mean joke.

"My . . . th-throat," he rasped, rubbing his neck.

"We're even," I said. "I just paid you back for telling me to bring wildflowers to Mrs. Maaargh."

"Wh-what was that?" he gasped. He opened another water bottle and started to drink.

"It's hot sauce," I said. "*Bombs Away!* hot sauce." I held the label up so he could see it. It showed a big explosion, and it read: IT EXPLODES IN YOUR MOUTH!

Ricardo was still panting like a dog. "You *like* that stuff?"

"No," I said. "I don't like it. But my whole family is nuts about hot sauce, even my little sister."

I made sure the cap was on tight. "They put it on everything," I said. "I mean everything, from morning to night. Pancakes, sandwiches, everything. I'm not kidding. They drink it straight from the bottle."

"Ow," Ricardo said, rubbing his throat. "But you hate it?"

"Yes, hate it," I said. "It burns my tongue and makes my whole head hurt."

Ricardo squinted at me. "So, if you hate it so much, why did they put it in your duffel bag?"

I shoved the bottle back in the duffel bag. "Because my dad says I won't be a man till I put hot sauce on my food. My whole family gives me a hard time about it. They call me a wimp because I eat my food without hot sauce."

"And they packed it in your bag because —?"

"Because I'm supposed to learn to be tougher here. It's Camp Winner, right? I'm supposed to man up and start using the stuff. So they packed it even though they know I hate it."

He nodded. He finished off the second water bottle.

I pointed to the hot sauce bottle. "Want some more?"

"You're joking, right? Get rid of that stuff. It's poison!" Ricardo declared.

I tucked the duffel bag under my cot. Then I sat down across from Ricardo. "Hey, listen," I said. "Now that we're even, don't you think we should help each other?"

He scrunched up his face, thinking about it. He brushed back his long dark hair. "Well . . . okay," he said finally. "You're a good dude. I'd really hate to see that monster eat you."

"So we'll help each other?" I asked.

"Yes," he replied. "You know about Bat Run Night — don't you?"

I shifted my weight on the cot. "Bat Run Night? What's that?"

"Mrs. Maaargh takes us all out late at night. Turns on lights. And a million bats come flying out of the woods and bombard us." He grinned. "Sound like fun?"

"Not exactly," I said.

"You get covered in bats," Ricardo said. "If you're lucky, they don't bite you."

"And the last camper standing is the winner?" I said.

"It's not quite that bad. But it's bad," he replied.

"How do you know about it?" I asked.

"My brother, Frederick, told me about it," Ricardo answered. "He was here two years ago." He sighed. "I told you, my family is very competitive."

He reached under the bed and pulled out a spray can. "Frederick told me a trick for Bat Run Night."

I studied the can. "What is that? Bug spray?"

He nodded. "Yeah. Frederick said you take this stuff and spray a whole mess of it in your hair. He said bats hate it."

"Bug spray?" I said. "Bats hate bug spray?"

"Yeah. You spray it in your hair and bats won't bother you. Frederick said they'll fly *away* from you. And just cling to everyone else."

He tossed the can to me. "Do it, Tommy. And you won't be the loser tonight. Mrs. Maaargh will have to move you up on her chart." He trotted to the door.

"Where are you going?" I asked.

"I'm late. I'm in the tetherball tournament," he said. "I know I can win it. My dad set up a tetherball pole in our backyard, and I practiced all spring."

The door slammed behind him. I watched him trot down the hill. *He says he doesn't like to compete*, I thought. *But that's a lie. He's a real win-win dude.*

I studied the can of bug spray in my hand. Should I spray it in my hair before tonight?

That was the big question. Was Ricardo really trying to help me? Or was this another trick?

24

The tall bonfire crackled. The flames danced up against a black sky.

There was no breeze at all. I could feel the heat of the fire on my face. Behind the wall of fire, the woods were silent. Even the crickets were quiet tonight.

We were all called from our cabins at ten o'clock. Counselors led us down the hills to the edge of the woods.

The fire had already been lit when we came down. The twigs and branches were already red-hot. We could see the blurred outlines of trees behind the fire.

Uncle Felix moved back and forth in front of the bonfire. It was a warm night, and the fire sent rays of heat over all of us. But he was dressed in a down vest and wool cap.

He scurried about, lining everyone up in a straight line. Girl campers to the left, boys to the right. We all stood facing the fire and the woods.

89

Some branches crackled and dropped, sending up bright yellow sparks. I took a deep breath. The fire smelled smoky and sharp. I love that smell.

But I couldn't enjoy it tonight. I knew what was about to happen.

Mrs. Maaargh stepped in front of the fire. The woods seemed to grow darker. She was so wide, she blocked a lot of the light.

She raised a megaphone to her mouth. "Bat Run Night is one of my favorite parts of your Final Exam. Tonight is a true test of courage!" she boomed. "It's so much fun for me to watch you all being attacked by hundreds of bats."

She tossed back her head and laughed. Her laughter sounded like loud vomiting. "Just don't let the bats chew off too much of your flesh!" she cried. "I need you to save it for me!"

Was she staring at me when she said that? Yes!

"The bats of Winner Island have little prey. They are hungry. Hungry for blood." She licked her enormous lips.

A cold shiver went down my back. In the flickering light, I spotted Sophie in the middle of the girls. She had her arms crossed in front of her and was hopping up and down. I couldn't tell if she was excited or scared.

When she saw me, she smiled and flashed me a thumbs-up.

All I felt was heavy, shuddering dread. Call me weird. But I really don't like the idea of dozens of hungry bats swooping out of the woods at me.

"Remember, dogs," Mrs. Maaargh continued, shouting into the blaring megaphone, "when the bats fly at you, you must show courage. Do not move or flinch or try to duck away from them."

Wind swirled around the tall bonfire. The twigs and branches snapped in the heat.

"If you are at the bottom of my chart," she continued, "you can move yourself up by being brave. Stand perfectly still. Stare the bats in the eye — like a winner!"

Her hair flew behind her in the wind. "I'll be watching!" she boomed. "And always remember — I'm a lot hungrier than the bats! Hahahahaha!"

She lowered the megaphone and gave it to Uncle Felix. He raised it to his mouth and tried to say something. But the megaphone only let out squeals and squeaks. Finally, he gave up and set it down on the ground.

He fumbled with the whistle around his neck. Everyone tensed as he blew a long, shrill blast.

I felt all my muscles tighten. My throat closed up. It was suddenly hard to breathe.

Two spotlights flashed on. Bright beams of

91

light swept up and down over the treetops. Small shadows flickered in the lights. I heard the flap of wings. High-pitched screeches. The shadows grew larger.

"Here they come!" Uncle Felix shouted.

25

Frozen in fear, I stared into the sweeping lights. I watched the shadows grow. Bat shadows.

In seconds, I could see their flapping wings. They darted low, then swooped high again as the lights brought them soaring out of the trees.

They screeched and hissed, so loud they drowned out the crackle and roar of the bonfire. And as they came flapping around the sides of the fire, I could see their red eyes. Tiny red beams of glowing light. Angry eyes. Hungry eyes.

Bats swooped low over the line of kids. The flap of their wings drummed in my ears.

I saw some girls try to duck away. One boy down the line fell to his knees with a shout. But most kids didn't move.

The bats rose up again, screeching like angry cats. Then they dove.

"Noooo!" I couldn't help it. I cried out as a flapping bat landed in my hair. Its talons dug into my scalp.

I swung my hands and tried to slap it off my head. But another bat, an even bigger one, dropped onto my shoulder. Its angry cries rang in my ear.

I bent and squirmed, slapping at it. But it dug into my shoulder.

I staggered away from the line of kids as two more bats thudded heavily onto my back. I fell to my knees, swatting and slapping at them.

But the more I fought, the harder they clung to me, wings flapping, red eyes staring so angrily, screeching and hissing all around me.

As I struggled to fight them off, I glimpsed the other kids. The long line of campers. They all stood perfectly still, eyes on the woods. No bats on them. The bats were ignoring them all.

I sprawled flat on my back now as a dozen bats clawed and snapped at me, flapping over my entire body.

Suddenly, Ricardo's face loomed above me. "Tommy —" he whispered. "The bug spray! Didn't you use the bug spray?"

"N-no," I choked out. "I didn't trust you. I thought it was another trick."

Ricardo shook his head. "But I was trying to *help* you this time. We all used it!"

He disappeared from view as furry, warm bats covered my face.

The next thing I knew, Mrs. Maaargh was brushing the bats off me easily with her enormous clawed paws. She slapped and swiped at them and sent them flying back to the trees.

Then she bent over me, gobs of drool plopping from her open mouth. "I see you're the only one who didn't get the word to use the bug spray," she said. She tsk-tsked. "You messed up again, didn't you?"

I tried to reply, but I could only groan.

"The bats think you're delicious, Tommy," she growled. "I'm sure I will, too."

26

Could I get to sleep that night? Three guesses — and all of them are *no*.

For one thing, my skin still itched like crazy and my head and hair tingled. I felt as if the bats were still on me. Still digging into my skin and scratching at me.

Every time I closed my eyes, I saw flapping bat wings. Red eyes. Sharp talons digging into my skin.

I tried sleeping on one side, then the other. Then I tried sleeping on my stomach with the pillow over my head. No way I could get comfortable. No way I could shut off my brain.

Ricardo snored gently in his cot across the cabin. He had no worries. He was near the top of the chart. He wasn't going to be monster food in a few days.

I gazed through the dark at Ricardo, his blanket pulled over his chin. He really had tried to help me. He gave me the bug spray so I wouldn't get covered in bats.

He told me the truth.

Did that mean I could trust him now?

I knew I couldn't trust Sophie. But I was wrong about Ricardo.

If only I had listened to him . . .

I turned onto my back and stared up at the ceiling. Outside the window, an owl hooted in a faraway tree.

A million questions flashed through my mind. Could I survive even with Ricardo's help? Did I stand the tiniest chance of climbing up from the bottom of Mrs. Maaargh's chart?

Or was I doomed before I even took the next two parts of The Teacher's Final Exam?

I sat up on the cot, wide awake. I couldn't stop myself. I crossed the cabin and shook Ricardo awake.

He groaned. "Hey, what's up?"

"Tell me about the next part of the exam," I said.

He blinked several times, still half asleep. "The next part?"

"Your brother took it, right? What did he say? What do we have to do?"

Ricardo sat up and stretched his arms above his head. He squinted hard at me. "You know, I can get in major trouble if I'm caught trying to help you."

"You won't get caught," I said. "No way." I shook him by the shoulders. "Give me a break. You know I'm *doomed* if you don't help me."

"Okay, okay." He pushed me away. "Don't totally lose it, Tommy." He took a long drink from a water bottle. "I'll tell you what comes next."

I was too worked up to sit still. I started to pace back and forth the length of the cabin.

"The next part is the underground swim," Ricardo said.

"The *what*?"

"There are these underground caves on the other side of the island," Ricardo continued. "It's pitch-black inside them. Lake water flows like a river through the caves. It twists and turns and curves around. We have to swim through the water to the end of the underground caves, see."

I stopped pacing. "You mean in total darkness?"

He nodded. "My brother said you can't see a thing. You can't even see the cave walls. That's how dark it is. But somehow you have to swim to the end."

I shuddered. "That's impossible. If you can't see where you're going . . ."

Ricardo grinned. "Here's the trick." He pulled something out from under his bed. It looked like a fat pen. "Tuck this into your swimsuit. It's a penlight. See? You click it here."

He pushed one end, and a light flashed on at the other end.

"Wow. Pretty bright," I said.

"Bright enough to see where you're going," he said. "Here." He reached under the bed again and pulled out another light. He handed it to me. "Remember, tuck it into your suit before we leave for the caves. My brother said it's the only way you can finish the swim test."

I thanked him and walked back to my cot. I felt a little more relaxed. Maybe I could get to sleep now.

I lay on my back and rolled the penlight between my hands. I felt sure that Ricardo really was trying to help me again. I believed he was being a good friend.

Could I really save myself now? Could I swim my way up from the bottom of the chart?

27

"You must stay alert," Mrs. Maaargh said. "The cave walls are jagged and sharp. Don't try to swim in a straight line. You'll swim right into the wall and cut yourself. I don't like my meat shredded. So follow the water as it curves."

She stood at the mouth of the first cave. A muddy path led down to the underground river that curled through the dark caverns.

There were five guys gazing at the blackness beyond the cave opening. Mrs. Maaargh was taking five of us at a time for this part of the exam. Ricardo and I got separated. I was on my own with four other dudes I didn't know.

I kept feeling the penlight tucked under my swim trunks. Making sure it hadn't fallen out.

Every time my fingers wrapped around it, I felt a little better.

I can do this. I can definitely pass this part of the test.

"This is a real survival test," Mrs. Maaargh said. "A winner can survive this. A winner can find his way through the darkest of waters. A loser will have to be dragged out."

She turned and stared at me. "A loser will have to be *eaten*."

Then she tossed her head back and laughed her loud, ugly laugh that echoed again and again in the dark caves.

She waved us into the cave. "Single file," she ordered. "One at a time. Try to ignore the smell down there. There are a lot of rotting corpses of river creatures you don't want to think about."

That sent a cold tingle down my back.

Two counselors in swim trunks stood on either side of the cave opening. I recognized one of them — my old mud-tag friend, Bert.

"If you get in trouble, scream your head off," he said. "Your shouts will echo through the caves. Maybe I'll be able to find you and rescue you in time."

Maybe?

Another shiver. And then my bare feet were sinking into the soft mud of the path. I was first in line, leading the way down.

The air temperature suddenly dropped twenty degrees. A sharp smell rose to my nostrils, nearly choking me. Cold water lapped over my ankles.

I could see the start of the underground river ahead of me. In the dim light, the water was a soupy dark green. I kept walking. The cold water climbed up to my knees.

I could hear the splash of the four dudes' footsteps behind me as they followed me into the darkness of the cave. No one spoke.

I kept my eyes straight ahead as the cave grew wider and the light from outside faded. "Ohhh!" I let out a cry as I stepped forward and my foot touched . . . *nothing.*

The river floor dipped without warning. I sank into the cold water. It rose rapidly over my waist and up to my shoulders. Was I going to sink under the surface?

I didn't wait to find out. I pushed my arms forward and started to swim. The current pulled me forward, forcing me to pick up speed. I could hear the splashing strokes of the four other guys echoing off the cave walls.

Just as the final rays of sunlight vanished, I glimpsed a stone shelf jutting over the water. I ducked just in time. If I hadn't seen it, I probably would have cracked my head open on its edge.

My face in the water, I edged under the stone ledge, pulling myself with steady strokes. I'm not a bad swimmer. In fact, swimming is my best sport.

I'm on the sixth-grade swim team, and I do pretty well. Not well enough for my parents, of course. They think I should break every record and win every match.

I'm a pretty steady swimmer. But I never had to swim in pitch-blackness before.

I slowed my strokes. I squinted straight ahead. Flashes of green-yellow light washed down from up above. Just enough to see that the river curved and grew narrow as it flowed into another cave.

I let the current pull me.

Relax. Relax. The word kept repeating in my mind. But, of course, there was no way to relax. And, relaxing would have been the *worst* thing I could do. I had to stay alert.

The water grew warmer suddenly. A long shaft of sunlight sparkled up ahead of me. I could see the rock walls curve, and I followed the curve.

Not bad so far. I glanced back to see how the others were doing — and gasped.

Where were they?

I squinted into the ripples of light on the river surface. I raised my eyes to the wide opening of the cave I'd just come through. "Whoa."

No sign of them.

Did they get lost? Or did I swim the wrong way?

"Hey!" I shouted. My voice echoed again and again. I treaded water, listening for a reply. I watched for them to come following me into this new, narrow passage.

"Hey! Where are you guys?" My voice trembled, and my echoes trembled, too.

I'm all alone here, I realized.

I floated into a rapid whirlpool that spun me around. The sunlight vanished. Total blackness now. And here I was all by myself, spinning in a circle in the dark.

My chest tightened in panic. I froze, struggling to breathe normally.

Now what?

28

The water swirled me around. Fighting away my panic, I forced myself to move.

I ducked my head under the water, gave a hard push forward — and struggled against the force of the whirlpool.

Yes!

I pulled myself out of its grip. My head spun. I gazed around. In the dim light, I couldn't figure out which direction to swim.

But the current of the underground river didn't give me much choice. I couldn't fight it. It carried me forward, picking up speed. I let it carry me around another bend. Then the water dropped down a steep slope.

Like a roller-coaster ride, I thought.

Yes. This was like one of those scary swim rides at a water park. Not my favorite thing. My family loves them. But I —

"Hey!"

I splashed to the bottom, hit hard — and found myself tossed up, then back. The river rocked hard, pushing me around, lifting me, then dropping me.

I struggled to see the cave walls. If the tossing waves slammed me into the side, I could be cut to pieces.

There was no light here. No way to see.

"Hey! Can anyone hear me?" I tried to shout. But a tall wave filled my mouth with water. I started to choke. The water tasted like puke.

Another wave spun me around. Struggling to swim, I was shoved against a cave wall. It was smooth, at least. But the hard bump sent a shudder of fear that tightened my muscles.

The penlight. I finally remembered the penlight in my trunks.

Tossed up, then down in the rough waters, I reached for it.

Don't drop it. Whatever you do . . .

I wrapped my fingers around it tightly, pulled it up, and held it in front of me.

I really needed it now. I needed to see what was up ahead. I needed it to find a way out of this rocking, rough water.

I slid the pen in my hand. Aimed it in front of me. And used my thumb to push the button on the back.

Nothing. No light.

I let out a groan. I pushed the button again. No. Nothing.

"Oh, wow."

A wave shoved my shoulder into the cave wall again. I pushed the back of the pen harder. Pushed it again. I shook it hard. Then pressed it again.

No. No light. The penlight didn't work.

I shook it again — and the top flew off. I raised it to my face and squinted inside it.

No batteries. The penlight was empty. No batteries.

Ricardo, you did it to me again!

A hard wave smacked my back into the rocky cave wall. I careened off, my back throbbing — and started to scream for help.

29

My scream rang off the cavern walls. I screamed again. Screamed till my voice was hoarse and my throat ached.

No one is coming for me. I'm stuck in here.

Finally, I heard splashing. Someone swimming steadily toward me.

Bert! I could see his bald head in the gray light. He looked like a big porpoise. He wrapped an arm around my waist and began to tug me out of the cavern.

That was my final exam. A total fail.

The other four guys did okay. They all made it to the end.

Why did they disappear behind me? Why did I end up all alone in the dark waters?

"Dog, you missed the very first turn," Bert explained. "You swam into the wrong cavern. Dude, you were doomed from the start."

Doomed was definitely my word of the summer.

I'd never had a fistfight in my life. But as Bert led me back to camp, I pictured myself fighting Ricardo . . . punching him until he begged me to forgive him.

Maybe Camp Winner was toughening me up, after all.

He was in one of the last swim groups. So I didn't see him till dinner.

As soon as he walked into the dining hall, I jumped up from my chair and ran up to him. I had both fists tightly balled up. But I didn't swing them at him.

He acted innocent. "Tommy, how'd you do?" he asked.

"Huh?" I cried. I could feel my face turning red with anger. "How did I do? How do you *think* I did?"

He shrugged. His hair was still wet. He had a scratch on one shoulder. Probably from a cave wall. "I heard you missed the first turn."

"Forget the first turn," I said through gritted teeth. "The penlight didn't work, Ricardo. It didn't work. It didn't help me."

His eyes went wide. I grabbed his shoulder. "Don't act surprised. I know what you did. You tricked me again."

"No way!" he cried. He pulled his shoulder free. "No way. I gave you that pen to help you in the caves, Tommy. No way it was a trick."

I shook both fists in the air. "There were no

109

batteries in the penlight," I said. "It was totally empty."

Ricardo blinked a few times. He backed away from me. "I had two lights, remember? One for me and one for you. I thought they both had batteries. Wow." He shook his head. "I'm so sorry, Tommy. Seriously. We should have tested them both."

"You're a liar," I said. "You gave me the one without batteries because you wanted to win."

"Not true," he insisted. "I wanted to help you. I wanted to save your life. Do you know what will happen to me if Mrs. Maaargh finds out I tried to help you?"

I didn't answer. I stared at him, studying his face. I was trying to decide if he was telling the truth.

I couldn't decide.

I turned and saw Mrs. Maaargh rumbling into the dining hall.

"I'll help you with the last part of the Final Exam," Ricardo whispered. "I promise. This time we'll make sure you're safe."

He spun away and trotted to the food table. He didn't want Mrs. Maaargh to see him talking to me.

Again, my head was spinning. I didn't know what to believe.

There was only one more part of the test. Was there any way at all I could move myself up on the chart and save my life?

Mrs. Maaargh rumbled to the front of the room. She clapped her huge baseball-mitt hands over her head. The room immediately grew silent.

She grabbed a whole chicken off the food table and stuffed it into her mouth. Her chewing sounds reminded me of a garbage truck grinding up trash. Finally, she swallowed the chicken with a loud *gulllllp.*

"I think we should all give a hand to Sophie!" she shouted, burping as she talked. "Sophie won the underground swim today!"

Everyone obediently clapped.

I saw Sophie at one of the girls' tables. She stood up and pumped her hands above her head like a boxing champion. She had a big grin on her face.

And why shouldn't she? She was safe now. She probably moved to the top of Mrs. Maaargh's chart.

I started back to the table. But Mrs. Maaargh pointed at me and waved her finger to call me over. I had no choice. I slumped over to her.

She had chicken grease smeared over her fat, flabby face. "Tommy, don't fall in the quicksand pit tomorrow, okay?" she growled.

My mouth dropped open. "Huh? Quicksand?"

She nodded. "Yeah. Don't fall in, okay? All that gritty sand gets stuck in my teeth."

30

After breakfast the next morning, Uncle Felix, Mrs. Maaargh, and all the counselors led everyone to the High Cliffs and the quicksand pit below them.

It was a long walk in the hot sun to the other side of the island. Then a steep climb up a sloping hill that led to the High Cliffs.

No one spoke. No one whispered or laughed or made a sound.

We all knew how serious this was. Especially me.

The final part of the Final Exam. The last chance to decide who was going home a winner. And who was staying on the island — as *dinner*!

I knew kids were watching me as we walked. I caught them staring. They looked away when I saw them. I knew what they were thinking. They were feeling sorry for Tommy the Loser. And they were also feeling glad that they weren't me.

Maybe I'll surprise them, I told myself. *Maybe I've been waiting for the final challenge to prove I'm a winner.*

Maybe.

Sweat prickled the back of my neck. I slapped a mosquito off my arm.

We climbed the grassy hill in silence. I saw Sophie at the head of the line, walking behind Mrs. Maaargh.

Sophie knew she was a winner. Her name was now at the top of Mrs. Maaargh's chart. But Sophie had the same tense, worried expression as the rest of us.

Everyone knew the final part of the Final Exam would be dangerous and terrifying. And as I reached the top of the hill and saw the twin cliffs and the wide orange quicksand pit so far below, I knew this was about to be the most frightening moment of my life.

The two dark-rock cliffs jutted out, facing each other. I'd say they were at least twenty feet apart.

A wooden ladder had been placed between the two cliffs. Like a bridge connecting them.

And down below . . . way down below . . . I could see the quicksand pit Mrs. Maaargh had warned about. Even from this high up, I could see it bubbling and tossing like a thick ocean.

Seeing the ladder stretching between the cliffs, I had a pretty good idea of what we were supposed to do to pass the test. But Mrs. Maaargh stepped up to the cliff edge to explain.

"This is the easiest test yet!" she exclaimed. Then she burst out laughing. "Well . . . maybe it isn't as easy as it looks. But it will separate the winners from the loser."

She gazed at me as she said the word *loser*.

"You get down on your hands and knees," she continued. "And you climb across the ladder, one rung at a time. Take your time. Move across the ladder as slowly as you like."

A gust of wind made the ladder bounce. It didn't look very sturdy to me.

"Grip the rungs carefully," Mrs. Maaargh instructed. "One slip — and you will plunge headfirst into the quicksand pit down below."

Sophie raised her hand and waved it hard to get Mrs. Maaargh's attention. "If we fall into the pit," Sophie said in a trembling voice, "is there someone down there to fish us out?"

Mrs. Maaargh grinned at her. "Probably," she answered. Then she laughed again. Her laugh sounded like deep stomach belches.

Uncle Felix stepped forward to give us his usual pep talk. He was dressed in tennis whites, a white shirt, and shorts. And he swung a tennis racket as he talked.

"The Final Exam is a wonderful chance to show how Camp Winner has turned you into a winner!" he shouted in his high, shrill voice.

114

"Remember, everyone, a winner never falls — and a faller never wins! Think before you sink!"

Maybe he expected everyone to applaud after that. But we all just stood there in silence. Most of us had our eyes on the slender ladder stretched between the cliffs.

The sun beamed down. My hands were sweaty from the heat. What if they slipped off the ladder?

Before I could think about it more, Mrs. Maaargh stepped forward and made the most frightening announcement of all.

She had her bulging, tennis ball eyes on me as she started to talk. And the grin on her face told me she did not have good news for me.

"We are going to go across the ladder in order this morning," she boomed. She raised her Wait Watchers Chart in both hands. "We will begin with the camper at the *bottom* of the chart and go up."

My mouth suddenly went dry. It wasn't hard to figure out what that meant. It meant I had to go first.

"If anyone falls into the pit," Mrs. Maaargh continued, "the test is over. That camper is the loser. No one else has to try."

Now everyone was *definitely* staring at me. The other kids all knew that if I fell, they'd be totally safe. They wouldn't have to crawl over the pit. They could go back to camp and celebrate.

115

I knew their eyes were all on me. It made me angry. Did everyone here really think I was a total loser?

Mrs. Maaargh beckoned me forward with one black-taloned finger. I stepped to the edge of the cliff. "This looks too easy!" I said, loud enough so everyone could hear. "Don't you have anything more challenging for a Final Exam?"

I managed to say that without my voice trembling and giving me away. I felt good. Why should I let everyone see how totally terrified I was?

I dropped onto my hands and knees. I crawled to the cliff edge.

I peered down at the bubbling quicksand pit so far below. I'd never had trouble with heights before. But I sure did now!

Sunlight flashed in my eyes. I suddenly felt dizzy. My legs were trembling so hard, I couldn't make them crawl to the ladder.

"Get going, dog," Mrs. Maaargh growled.

I took a deep breath and held it. But it didn't help slow my racing heartbeats.

My hands shaking, I leaned down and grabbed the first rung of the ladder. My hands were wet with sweat. I gripped the rung as tightly as I could and crawled forward a few inches.

Then I reached out carefully and grabbed the second rung.

Silence all around. I knew the campers were all watching with their fingers crossed. Somewhere a bird hooted in a faraway tree.

I glanced back. Mrs. Maaargh wasn't even watching. She had turned her back to talk to Uncle Felix.

I reached for the third rung — but stopped when a hand gripped my ankle.

"Wait —" Ricardo whispered.

31

I gripped the third rung. My knee pushed into the first rung. I was already out over the side of the cliff. I swung my head around to Ricardo. "What do you want?"

"The tenth rung is a fake," he whispered. He glanced back to make sure Mrs. Maaargh didn't see him.

"What do you mean?" I demanded.

"Don't grab the tenth rung," he warned. "If you grab the tenth one, it will break off — and you'll fall into the quicksand."

"How — how do you know?" I stammered.

"I heard two counselors talking after breakfast. They said Mrs. Maaargh made the tenth rung loose so it would break off."

I squinted at him. "You're sure?"

"I heard them," he insisted. "They said the tenth rung."

Ricardo jumped back just in time. Mrs.

Maaargh finished talking with Uncle Felix and turned to watch me on the ladder. Ricardo quickly backed away into the crowd of kids.

I took another deep breath. My hands were dripping wet. But no way I could stop to wipe them off on my shirt or anything.

I grabbed the fourth rung and slid my knees forward. I was out over the quicksand pit now. I knew I couldn't back up. I had to keep going.

And I had to remember . . . *Don't grab the tenth rung.*

"Ow." The hard wooden rungs made my knees ache. The sun beat down on me. The sunlight made it hard to focus my eyes.

I wrapped my hands around the fifth rung.

Don't grab the tenth one. Go right to the eleventh rung.

Skip the tenth one. Skip the tenth one.

A sharp pain tightened my back. I ignored it and grabbed the sixth rung.

The wind gusts seemed to grow stronger as I climbed farther between the two cliffs. The ladder bounced beneath me.

I grabbed the seventh rung. Pulled myself forward.

I took another deep breath. I tried to swallow but my mouth was too dry.

I waited for the wind to fade. Then I squeezed my hand around the eighth rung.

It broke off with a loud *craaaaaaack*.

My hands fluttered like birds as I fell forward, fell from the ladder. Plunged headfirst.

Headfirst. Down . . . down . . . screaming all the way.

32

My scream cut off as I did a hard belly flop into the quicksand. My face hit the sand first. It was burning hot!

My body smacked the surface of the wet sand, and I sank instantly.

I raised my hands and tried to slap the surface. But that didn't help. The thick, wet sand rose up as if swallowing me. And sucked me down.

I couldn't breathe. I couldn't see. I struggled to kick my legs and push myself to the surface.

As I struggled and kicked and squirmed and pulled, I thought about Ricardo.

Dog-eat-dog. Eat or be eaten.

Ricardo tricked me so he wouldn't have to go across the ladder. He tricked me — and I fell for it.

Kids like Ricardo came to this camp to compete and defeat everyone else. They came to win,

win, win. And I just never caught on. I trusted him to the very last moment.

A burst of anger made me thrust myself forward with my arms and legs. I kicked hard in the burning, thick sand — and gasped when my head poked up over the surface.

I tilted my head back and sucked in air. I raised my arms over the pit and kicked again, rising higher.

I heard a shout and saw Bert wading toward me. Bert to the rescue again. He grabbed my arm and pulled me up. Then he wrapped his arm around my waist and carried me out of the quicksand.

I rubbed sand off my face with both hands. "Guess the Final Exam is over," I said.

Mrs. Maaargh stared down at me, drooling. "Don't think of yourself as a loser, Tommy," she said. "Think of yourself as a *good meal.*"

33

Bert led me to the shower cabin. He forced me to take a very long shower. He reminded me that Mrs. Maaargh doesn't like sand in her food.

Standing under the shower, I tried to think. Could I come up with an escape plan? Was there any way I could save myself?

The hot water poured down on me. I stood there thinking for a long time, maybe twenty minutes. No ideas came to me.

Too late to try to contact my parents. Besides, I'd already tried that.

No place on the island to escape to. No place to hide. I'd tried that, too.

As Bert led me to my cabin, I sighed sadly. I knew I was doomed. The Final Exam was over, and I had failed. No way I could change my fate.

"Get dressed," Bert said. "We don't want to keep Mrs. Maaargh waiting. She likes her lunch on time." He patted my shoulder. "Sorry, kid. Really. What else can I say? Sorry."

He said he'd come back for me in a few minutes. I watched him walk down the hill.

I stepped into the cabin to get ready. I couldn't decide what to wear. What do you wear when you're about to be a monster's lunch?

I pulled on a Camp Winner T-shirt and my gym shorts. I was tying my sneakers when Sophie and Ricardo burst into the cabin.

"I didn't trick you. I swear!" Ricardo cried. "I heard those counselors say it was the tenth rung. Really. They probably knew I was listening. So they played a trick on me."

I squinted at him. I didn't want to believe him. I wanted to stay angry.

"He's telling the truth," Sophie insisted. "I know he wanted to help you. We both like you, Tommy. We wouldn't want —"

"The counselors tricked us," Ricardo said. "I wouldn't lie to you."

I sighed. "It's too late anyway," I murmured. "What difference does it make now?"

"You're a hero!" Sophie declared. "Really. You are. You saved the rest of us."

"Some hero," I muttered, rolling my eyes. "A hero *sandwich* is more like it."

"Everyone thinks you're a winner, Tommy," Ricardo said. "Just think of that. Everyone thinks you're a hero."

I opened my mouth to reply. But Bert knocked on the cabin door and stepped inside. His eyes were sad. But he blocked the door in case I tried to run away.

"You ready?" he asked softly.

"I . . . don't know how to answer that," I said.

I gave Sophie and Ricardo a fast wave. Then I followed Bert out the door.

As we walked down the path to the dining hall, I thought about breaking free and making a run for it.

Bert watched me and stayed close, as if he could read my mind.

A few minutes later, we walked into the back of the dining hall. Bert led me through the kitchen.

We walked past the stoves and the sinks. And then . . . I let out a sharp cry as I saw a huge silver serving platter, big enough for me to fit in tight and snug.

34

And now, here I was on my back. In just gym shorts. I was squeezed into the silver platter. My arms folded over my chest.

I gazed up at Mrs. Maaargh. She leaned over the table and drooled on me, wet yellow drool. She grinned and licked her liver lips with her fat tongue.

"I plan to eat your arms first," she said. "You know. Get the bony parts out of the way."

Was I supposed to say something? I crossed my arms tighter over my chest to stop from shaking.

"Don't worry, Tommy," she said. "I'll eat your head *last*."

Huh? Was that supposed to make me feel better? Was that *good news*?

She poked my ribs with a fat finger. "Mmmmmmm." She made disgusting lip-smacking sounds.

126

She leaned over me, drool running over her lower lip. She grabbed my right arm and pulled it toward her jagged teeth.

Nothing can save me now, I realized. *I can't believe this is how I end up — as a monster's lunch.*

I shut my eyes. I couldn't bear to watch.

I gritted my teeth and waited for the incredible pain.

Waited.

Then I opened my eyes in time to see her roll out her enormous, fat tongue. She brought my arm to her lips. And she ran her tongue up and down my arm. She LICKED me, a long, slow lick. Her tongue was rough and dry and felt like sandpaper on my skin.

LLLLLIIIIIIICCK.

Then her pointed teeth poked out as she opened her mouth wide to bite.

35

But she didn't bite down. Instead, a choked gasp escaped her throat.

Her eyes bulged. Her face darkened to purple.

"AAAAAAAAAACK." She stuck her tongue way out, and a hideous cry burst from her open mouth.

She dropped my arm. She fell back with a violent jerk of her whole body.

She started to gag and choke. Her huge body quivered and shook.

She gagged and gagged, wiping her tongue against her lips.

She turned back to me in horror. "My tongue! My whole mouth! It's BURNING! BURNING! What did you do? What did you DO?!"

I sat up in the platter.

She squeezed her throat and choked some more.

"It's my *Bombs Away!* hot sauce," I said. "I rubbed it all over me. It explodes in your mouth. Do you like it?"

She frantically waved her arms above her head and shrieked in pain. "Burning! BURNING! My mouth is ON FIRE! HELP ME! I'm DYING! I'm ON FIRE!"

Holding her throat, her tongue flapping the air, she spun away from the table — and ran out of the dining hall screaming at the top of her lungs.

I jumped out of the platter and lowered myself to the floor. I walked to the window and peered out. I could see Mrs. Maaargh down below. Running and screaming.

I could hear her through the open window. "I'm DYING! I'm BURNING! BURNING! Help me! I'm DYING!"

Pressing my face to the window glass, I watched her rocket across the beach. She didn't stop at the water. She plunged into the lake and kept running. And then she was swimming. Paddling furiously, swimming away.

Did she plan to swim across the whole lake? I watched her slap the water, kicking and splashing, sending up high waves, until she vanished in the distance.

Gone. Mrs. Maaargh was gone.

I stared out at the water for a long time. She didn't swim back.

A smile crossed my face. *My parents were right,* I thought. *A person can't live without hot sauce.*

36

"Party! Party! Par-tee!"

Kids chanted as music rocked the camp. We danced. We celebrated. We swam. We pulled all the cake and cookies and ice cream from the camp kitchen and had the biggest island party blowout in history.

Uncle Felix locked himself in his office. There was no way he could stop us.

Five more days of camp. Five more days of celebration and partying. No Mrs. Maaargh. No more dog-eat-dog competitions. We were all friends now.

I climbed up on a table in the dining hall and ripped Mrs. Maaargh's chart into tiny shreds. Then I tossed the shreds up like confetti. Everyone cheered and danced and sang.

"I knew you were a hero," Sophie said to me. "I told you so, didn't I?"

"Now we're *all* winners!" Ricardo exclaimed, slapping me on the back.

Bert and the other counselors partied with us. Everyone celebrated the fact that Mrs. Maaargh the monster had fled the island in a total panic.

Our party lasted for two whole days.

And then a new Teacher showed up.

Uncle Felix introduced him to everyone in the dining hall. "I don't know where he came from. But he just arrived, and I know you dogs will make him feel welcome."

He stepped aside — and a huge, ugly *two-headed* monster stepped forward.

We all groaned and stared in horror as the two heads began to speak.

"I am Mr. Baaargh," one head shouted.

The other head said, "I'll be The Teacher till the end of camp. And I don't want any of you to worry."

"Camp Winner will continue as normal," the first head said.

He pulled up a new chart. "Keep your eyes on the chart, everyone. At the end of camp, I'm going to eat two of you."

GOOSEBUMPS®
MOST WANTED

PLANET OF THE LAWN GNOMES

Here's a sneak peek!

I know I'm supposed to be careful. I know I'm supposed to be good. But sometimes you have to take a chance and hope no one is watching.

Otherwise, life would be totally boring, right?

My name is Jay Gardener. I'm twelve and sometimes I can't help it — I like a little excitement. I mean, dare me to do something — and it's done.

It's just the way I am. I'm not a bad dude. Sure, I'm in trouble a lot. I've been in some pretty bad trouble. But that doesn't mean I'm a criminal or anything.

Check out these big blue eyes. Are these the eyes of a criminal? No way. And my curly red hair? And the freckles on my nose? You might almost call me *cute*, right?

Okay, okay. Let's not get sickening about it.

My sister, Kayla, calls me Jay Bird because she says I'm as cute as a bird. Kayla is totally weird. Besides, she has the same red hair and blue eyes. So why pick on *me*?

So, okay, I felt this temptation come on. You know what that is. Just a strong feeling that you have to do something you maybe shouldn't do.

I gazed up and down our street. No one around. *Good.* No one to watch me.

The summer trees' leaves shimmered in the warm sunlight. The houses and lawns gleamed so bright, I had to squint. I stepped into the shade of Mr. McClatchy's front yard.

McClatchy lives in the big old house across the street from us. He's a mean dude and everyone hates him. He's bald and red-faced and as skinny as a toothpick. He wears his pants way up high so the belt is almost up to his armpits.

He yells at everyone in his high, shrill voice. He's always chasing kids off his lawn — even new kids, like Kayla and me. He's even mean to our dog, the sweetest golden Lab who ever lived — Mr. Phineas.

So, I had an idea to have a little fun. Of course it was wrong. Of *course* it wasn't what I was supposed to be doing. But sometimes, when you see something funny to do — you just have to take a chance.

Am I right?

That morning, I saw some guys in green uniforms doing work on the tall trees in McClatchy's front yard. When they went home, they left a ladder leaning against a tree.

I glanced up and down the street again. Still no one in sight.

I crept up to the ladder and grabbed its sides. I slid it away from the tree trunk. The ladder was tall but light. Not hard to move.

Gripping it tightly by the sides, I dragged it to the front of McClatchy's house. I leaned it against the wall. Then I slid it to the open window on the second floor.

Breathing hard, I wiped my sweaty hands on the legs of my jeans. "Sweet," I murmured. "When McClatchy comes home, he'll see the ladder leaning up against the open window. And he'll totally panic. He'll think a burglar broke into his house."

The idea made me laugh. I have a weird laugh. It sounds more like hiccupping than laughing. Whenever I laugh, my whole family starts to laugh because my laugh is so strange.

Well, actually, Mom and Dad haven't been laughing with me much lately. Maybe I've done some things that aren't funny. Maybe I've done some things I shouldn't have. That's why I had to promise to be good and stay out of trouble.

But the ladder against the open window was definitely funny. And it wasn't such a bad thing to do, right? Especially since McClatchy is the meanest, most-hated old dude in the neighborhood.

Still laughing about my joke, I turned and started down the driveway. McClatchy has a tall hedge along the bottom of his yard. It's like a wall. I guess he really wants to keep people out.

At the end of the driveway, his mailbox stood on a tilted pole. And as I passed it, I saw the trash cans in the street. The trash was bulging up under the lids — and it gave me another cool idea.

Working fast, I pulled open the mailbox, lifted the lid off a trash can — and started to stuff trash into McClatchy's mailbox.

Yes! A greasy bag of chicken bones. A crushed soup can. Some gooey yellow stuff that looked like puke. Wet newspapers. More soup cans.

I imagined McClatchy squeaking and squealing in his high voice when he opened the mailbox and found it jammed with disgusting garbage.

What a hoot.

I started to laugh again — but quickly stopped. A choking sound escaped my throat.

Whoa.

Someone watching me. *Two* people watching, half-hidden by the tall hedge.

I froze. They stood side by side, staring right at me. I knew they saw everything. *Everything.*

A chunk of moldy cheese and a clump of newspaper fell from my hands. I staggered back from the mailbox.

Caught. I was totally caught.

2

"Okay. You got me. I'm sorry," I called. "I'll clean it up. Right away."

I reached into the mailbox and started to pull out trash.

But the two men didn't reply. They stood staring at me. The hedge rustled in the breeze, making shadows quiver over their still faces.

"I'm cleaning it up," I called. "No problem."

It took me a few more seconds to realize they weren't people. And they weren't alive.

"Huh?" Crumpled soda cans fell from my hands and clattered to the driveway as I took a step toward them.

Lawn gnomes.

I burst out laughing when I realized what they were.

Jay, you just freaked out because you were caught by lawn gnomes!

Walking in the shadow of the tall hedge, I stepped up to them. I placed a hand on a pointed red cap and squeezed it. Solid plaster or something.

I poked the stony dude in the eyes. I pinched his hard cheeks. "How's it going, dudes? Lookin' good!"

Nearly as tall as me, they stood side by side in red vests over matching red overalls. Beneath their pointed red caps, they had shiny round faces with white beards and white mustaches.

Their eyes were big. One had brown eyes. The other had black. They had stubby, wide noses, almost like pig snouts. Their mouths were curled down in angry scowls.

Yes, angry. They looked angry. They weren't cute. They were mean looking and ugly. Their steady, cold gaze gave me a chill.

"Stop staring at me, dudes." I covered one gnome's eyes with my hand.

I had an idea. I danced back to the trash can. Then I placed a drippy soup can on the point of one gnome's red cap. And I draped a sheet of brown-stained newspaper over his partner's shoulder.

"Now you two look cool," I said.

I stepped back to the street and slammed the lid back on the trash can. Something caught my eye. Another lawn gnome standing under a tree in McClatchy's neighbor's yard.

I squinted at it for a moment. And spotted another angry-looking gnome near the neighbor's front walk. This one wore a blue cap. Its arms were straight out as if it were directing traffic.

Why do so many homes in this neighborhood have lawn gnomes?

My family moved here only three weeks ago. This was the first time I noticed them all.

I turned and gazed across the street at the Brickmans' house next door to ours. Yes. They had three lawn gnomes lined up along their driveway.

Totally weird.

I kicked a crushed soda can onto the grass. Then I moved forward and kicked it again. I stopped as a heavy shadow swept over me.

At first, I thought it was the shadow of the hedge. Or a tree.

But then I raised my eyes — and gasped.

McClatchy!

He grabbed me by the shoulders. His hands were bony hard, like skeleton hands. He lowered his red face to me and screamed in his shrill voice:

"I've been home the whole time. Watching you. What do we do with a troublemaker?"

3

McClatchy squeezed my shoulders in his bony hands. Then he let go of me. He was breathing hard, making whistling noises through his nose. His eyes bulged wide.

"S-sorry," I stammered.

"You're on my bad list now," McClatchy rasped. "And believe me, kid — you don't want to be on my bad list."

"Sorry," I repeated.

His eyes were on the open mailbox, jammed with trash. His shoulders shuddered. He kept making that whistling sound. Was he going to totally lose it?

I heard the scrape of footsteps. I turned toward them. "Oh, no!"

Now I was *really* in trouble. My dad came walking toward us. He had Mr. Phineas on his leash. "What's happening here?" Dad called.

Dad is tall and athletic looking. He has wavy brown hair and dark eyes and a great, gleaming smile. Mom calls him her "movie-star husband," I guess because he's kind of handsome.

He was in his workout clothes — a gray sleeveless T-shirt over gray sweatpants.

I lowered my head as he stepped up to us. Mr. Phineas sniffed furiously at the garbage that had fallen out of the can.

"Your son had better shape up," McClatchy said through clenched teeth.

I felt Dad's eyes on me. I kept my head down.

"What has Jay done?" Dad asked. "Did he spill this garbage?"

McClatchy motioned toward the house with his head. "He moved that ladder to the open window. I think he planned to sneak into my house."

Dad gasped.

"No way!" I screamed. "I just wanted you to think —"

"I'm sure Jay wouldn't break into your house," Dad told McClatchy.

"He didn't know I was home," McClatchy said. "I saw everything."

Dad put his hand on my chin and forced me to look at him. "Jay, did you plan to go into Mr. McClatchy's house?" he demanded.

I shook my head. "No way. Of course not."

He and McClatchy stared at me for a long while, as if I were some kind of lab specimen.

Dad spoke up first. "Jay hasn't been himself lately," he told McClatchy.

McClatchy just nodded. He kept rubbing his lips over his teeth, making a wet, smacky sound.

Dad picked up the soup can and dirty newspaper from the two lawn gnomes. He stuffed the garbage in the trash can. "Very sorry," he said softly. "It won't happen again. *Will* it, Jay?"

"No," I muttered.

Mr. Phineas was licking up something green and disgusting from the spilled trash. I tugged him away and pulled the green gunk from between his teeth. Then I followed Dad across the street.

He led me into the living room. "Have a seat." He pointed to the couch. Mr. Phineas had already plopped down on the rug in front of the fireplace.

I perched on the edge of the couch. "Are we going to have a serious talk now?" I said.

Dad stood above me. He frowned. "Son, tell me. Why are you acting so strange? You know you're not supposed to play tricks on the neighbors."

I smoothed my hand over the green leather arm of the couch. "Sorry, Dad," I murmured. "I . . . was just bored."

"Find things to do," Dad snapped. "I don't want you to get in any more trouble. Do you understand me?"

I nodded.

"You can spend the next five nights after dinner in your room," Dad said. "The next time, your punishment will be a lot worse."

"But, Dad —"

He shook his head angrily. Then he spun around and stomped angrily out of the living room.

Well, Jay, you messed up again.

I slumped back on the couch. I didn't want to make people angry at me. I just wanted to have some fun.

I called to Mr. Phineas to come over to me. I felt like petting him. But he wouldn't budge from his rug by the mantel. It's his favorite place.

Kayla walked into the room. "Don't tell me you're in trouble again, Jay."

"None of your business," I snapped.

She tossed back her curly red hair and sighed. "Nothing ever changes. We had to move because of you — and now you still act like a jerk in our new home."

"I already apologized," I muttered. "Maybe you could cut me some slack?"

She shrugged. "Let's go ride our bikes."

"Huh?" I climbed up off the couch.

"You heard me. Let's ride our bikes. There's a lot of stuff in this neighborhood we haven't seen yet."

"Yeah, okay," I agreed. "At least we can't get in trouble riding our bikes — right?"

Right?

About the Author

R.L. Stine's books are read all over the world. So far, his books have sold more than 300 million copies, making him one of the most popular children's authors in history. Besides Goosebumps, R.L. Stine has written the teen series Fear Street and the funny series Rotten School, as well as the Mostly Ghostly series, The Nightmare Room series, and the two-book thriller *Dangerous Girls*. R.L. Stine lives in New York with his wife, Jane, and Minnie, his King Charles spaniel. You can learn more about him at www.RLStine.com.

The Original Bone-Chilling Series

📖 SCHOLASTIC

www.scholastic.com/goosebumps